EMPIRE OF WOMEN

By
JOHN FLETCHER

I0616750

ARMCHAIR FICTION & MUSIC
PO Box 4369, Medford, Oregon 97504

*For more information about Armchair Books and products, visit our
website at…*

www.armchairfiction.com

Or email us at…

armchairfiction@yahoo.com

THE SECRETS TO ETERNAL LIFE...

That was the reward the men of Konapar were desperately looking for when they decided to stage an attack on the long-living women of the planet Phira. And it was this invasion scenario that one of the cagiest space pirates in the entire galaxy fell into. After encountering a mighty fleet of Konaparian warships, Captain Gan Alain and his indomitable crew were more or less "drafted" by the Regent of Konapar. Alain's vessel, the Warspear, *was to be a main support ship to the Regent as the attack on Phira commenced; for it was well known that nowhere in space was there a man who had the savvy and no-how of Captain Gan Alain. But fighting against women was something new to the Captain, and like wild horses, brutal men can be tamed—and greedy men can be bought!*

FOR A SECOND COMPLETE NOVEL, TURN TO PAGE 87

CAST OF
CHARACTERS

CAPTAIN GAN ALAIN
Pirate Captain, mercenary, business man. This guy knew what he wanted—and he knew how to get it!

CELYS
High priestess of the cult of Myrmi-Atla. She had reigned supreme for hundreds of years.

GUNNAR TOR BRANTHAK
The ambitious Regent of Konapar, he wanted the secret to eternal life and he would seize it at whatever the cost.

APHELE
Courageous and valiant, she was a warrior among the Phiran women. But she had dreams of a different way of life…

ELVIR
The bounty of a pirate raid. A ten-year-old, would-be slave, if not for the men who had found her.

CHAN DUCHAILE
First Mate on the Warspear. His loyalty to Captain Alain would never be in question.

THE ANCIENT ONE
One of the few women on Phira to show any signs of aging, she had been pitting her mind against men for 500 years!

CHAPTER ONE

THE *WARSPEAR* was loafing along under a half G acceleration somewhere between Denebola and Konapar, when the news tape started clicking out the story of the space battle that had served as a "declaration" of war between Konapar and Phira. The captain's hands reached for the controls, rang the acceleration alarm, and changed course. He upped the speed to a good ten G's.

Nobody takes that kind of acceleration if they can avoid it unless, like the Cap, they were raised on a two-G planet. Or unless there was a terrific reason which made it imperative, such as the reason in the Cap's mind as his eyes glittered in retrospection over the war news and what it implied.

The *Warspear* had to pass Phira within a half-hour's distance. But the Cap swung closer to the gigantic gray-green globe now, turning on the vari-wave detectors to pick up any vibration that might be disturbing the ether around Phira. There was a scramble of sound, but it was all in code and nothing he could make sense of, though he tried.

A few moments after the war news had come through on the tape, the radar screen picked up a ship, dead ahead, making for the atmosphere of Phira under full rocket blast. The Cap signaled her for identification. That he had no business asking made no difference to him. Apparently the strange ship knew that fact, for she refused to answer. The Cap leaned to his intercom.

"Mister DuChaile, put a torpedo across her bows," he said calmly.

Chan DuChaile was the first mate of the *Warspear*, and he deserved his post. Under his direction the torpedo crew put a

A shadow moved behind a pillar, and Cap's flash sent a quick beam of light toward it

guided missile across the stranger's bow so close the Cap
couldn't see space between the fiery wake and the hull. The

stranger's captain couldn't see it either, apparently, for he flashed a surrender signal immediately; not too surprisingly, because the *Warspear* could frighten almost anything in space

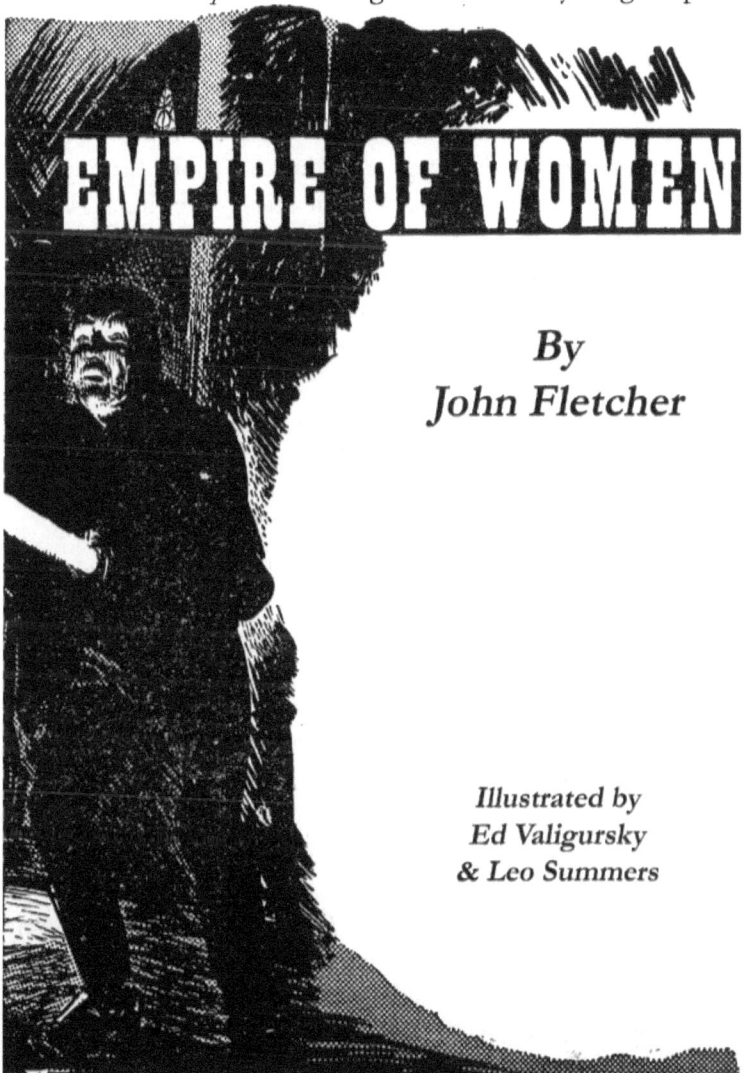

EMPIRE OF WOMEN

By
John Fletcher

Illustrated by
Ed Valigursky
& Leo Summers

into a collapse. Especially merchantmen, which this ship was, and which the *Warspear* was built for. In plain words, the

Warspear was a pirate.

When the prize crew boarded the captive they found to their delight that they had indeed captured a prize. She was loaded to the bulkheads with explosives, and a hundred tons of fission-grenades, designed to be thrown by repulse rays in hand weapons. These latter were outlawed wherever the Terran Empire held sway. It was a terrible weapon to place in a common soldier's hands, and the Cap looked thoughtful when the prize crew reported the cargo to him. If the Phirans had much of that type of weapon, they must mean business, outlawed business they didn't intend to allow any Terran to rule, or any code of decency to forestall. Alid, on Phira, was proving herself to be the barbarian nation she was!

For an instant the Cap chuckled. If he'd touched the other ship with just one ray, that cargo would have sent both ships to glory.

But he stopped chuckling when he learned of the forty-odd slave girls bound for the Temple of the Matriarchs in Alid. They had been branded already with the blue hieroglyph of Myrmi-Atla, which meant a strictly manless future for them, were they delivered to the infamous temple.

The Cap went over to the prize and looked at them. They were just kids, only beginning to blossom into maidenhood. Obviously the crew wanted to take them aboard, but the Cap knew better than that. He ordered them sent to the hideaway on the Black Moon.

But for the first time in his career, one of his orders was obeyed with questioning glances and a few mumbles of "it ain't fair"…for the Cap bent too long a glance on a sprightly little being he called "Elvir" because she was so small and quick. An "elvir" is a baby eel. She was a pert little blonde, not at all like an eel except for her smooth and quick movements, but the name seemed to fit all the same. Perhaps it was the way she accepted it, and the way she wriggled into the Cap's heart. Anyway, Elvir came aboard the *Warspear*, and jealousy shone out of the eyes of many of her crew. But it was a good kind of jealousy, for Elvir was only ten.

THE PRIZE crew boarded the freighter and headed her for the hideaway on the rock named the Black Moon…the Cap could always get quick cash out of a cargo of explosives. Then the *Warspear* resumed course for Konapar.

Before long, Elvir's pert beauty and high sense of humor had endeared her to everyone. She was full of questions, and she carried a potent load of sunbeams in her laugh and in her child's way of playing. The crew got a boost out of her, and she was too young to have to worry about any fights starting over her…or so the captain thought. Pirates his men might be, but there's a soft spot in the core of every real man, and the hardy fighters aboard the *Warspear* were no exception.

Elvir had never been to space before she had been placed aboard the freighter, and she was determined to learn all about it, which was funny because it was so impossible.

"Where are we, Captain Alain?" she'd ask, and he'd take her on his knee and trace out their course through the stars on the chart with one broad, scarred finger, and tell her a whopping big lie about the people of each planet along the course. She'd swallow it all and come back for more.

"What is the Empire of Terra? Who are the pirates you have to fight for Terra?" The Cap had reversed the truth and told her the *Warspear* was engaged in exterminating pirates. He'd patiently explain how huge the Terran Empire was, taking in a good portion of the galaxy, and how numberless the independent worlds where pirates could hang out masquerading as honest merchant ships. Little Elvir drank it all in, her eyes sparkling as she absorbed the star charts he handed her, and you'd swear she understood it all as well as he before a week was out.

"Will I meet some pirates?" she'd ask…and the Cap would look at Chan DuChaile and wink.

"I hope not," he'd say. "Pirates are terrible bad men!"

"What do pirates look like?" she'd ask, and he'd have them with long whiskers and blasters as big as beer kegs and bandy-legged and cross-eyed.

Chan and the other officers would laugh, but the fact was they themselves were about as war-scarred a bunch of mercenaries as ever looted a city or sacked a ship; and just about as deadly as any story-time pirate could hope to be.

But Captain Gan Alain had contacts, a reputation for straight dealing, and had turned in plenty of honest jobs convoying trading ships that had had sense enough to hire him. The rims of the Terran Empire were rough and tough, and most everything went. But most of the men on the *Warspear* knew the value of a good record on the official books, and especially did Gan Alain know this. He'd done convoying long enough for the traders to know he never doublecrossed an employer who paid his price.

There were others in the business, however, like Tiger Phelan, whose record included a half-dozen convoys that never reached port, and a dozen lame excuses by the Tiger as to where other cargoes had disappeared to—from his own holds. Men like the Tiger forced action against themselves by messing up the record. Out of a hundred trips, it was natural to lose one or two convoys. But it would be a very dumb and blind trader who hired the Tiger to take him across the void from Dires to Delphon.

On the record, the Cap's nose was clean. He could cradle at almost any civilized port without a murmur from officialdom. So far, that is…

ELVIR was either well developed for her age, or had adult instincts, for she fell for the captain. There was some excuse, for he *was* the kind most women make fools of themselves over. Full of vitality, ruddy-cheeked, curly-haired, he was taller and broader than most men of Earth stock. He'd been raised on a heavy planet, though he never talked much about exactly where it had been, and what kind of a home he'd had. On the *Warspear* everyone had secrets and sore spots—that's why they were there.

Captain Alain he was called, formally. In space some were allowed to call him "Cap", and a few called him Gan, off duty. He was a mild enough man, ordinarily; but so powerful that the mildness was deceptive. He didn't have to shout or bluster or throw his weight around to get obedience. His men had seen him break a man's back by hitting him in the belly in a fight, and they didn't give him any arguments. Big he was, with his mane of red-gold hair and beard making him look even bigger. Nobody pushed the Cap around. He could let out a bellow that made the plates in the hull rattle, but he seldom did. It wasn't necessary. Men leaped to obey his quietest whisper.

He was no ladies' man, but when there were ladies present, they did their best to make one out of him. Now little Elvir was on the same course, but somehow with her it was comical, she was so small. In spite of his attitude toward females, the Cap made a fuss over her; and so did all the rest, but without the reaction she gave the Cap.

CHAPTER TWO

IT WAS mid-course between Phira and Konapar that the radar beams began to have grasshoppers. The telescope finally gave the answer: they were heading smack into a whopping big fleet, as DuChaile put it.

The Cap began to decelerate, then turned the controls over to Chan. Most of the crew guessed what was ahead, but if they'd suspected their captain was planning on plunging right into the middle of the Konapar war fleet, they'd have worried a lot more than they did.

Soon the fleet became visible, strung out in a series of V's too numerous to count. There were hundreds of them and, as they neared, the televisor began to bellow out questions at the *Warspear*. When the crew heard their captain's answer, they suddenly had reason to worry, and most of the officers felt sure this was IT—the lugubrious finish of the *Warspear's* career. But every man stood to his post, grimly ready.

"Tell your commander this ship is the *Warspear*, heavy-cruiser class, with five-score seasoned fighting men, reporting for action against the Phiran tyranny."

Chan DuChaile, listening, had never heard the government of the Matriarchs called a tyranny before, and he didn't like the idea of fighting against women; but he knew Gan Alain well enough to realize there were wits at work, so he listened without too much amazement.

After a few seconds, the receiving screen came to life. Mentally, Chan analyzed the scene in his own peculiar way: A big, black-bearded mogul in a monkey-suit trimmed with gold braid, garnished with medals, draped with golden spaghetti and epaulettes. Chan recognized him, after a snort of disdain, as the Regent of Konapar. He'd seen his picture in a dozen bars in ports across the Dires sun-cluster.

Yet, after a good look at him, Chan wouldn't have given more than two brass buttons for the young prince's chances of ever taking over the rule of Konapar from this fellow. He was neither bad looking nor particularly villainish in appearance; it was just that he was a man who got what he wanted, and who wanted everything. Too ambitious, Chan classified him.

He was big-necked, big chested, black-haired, a very handsome man. His cheeks were a little too full and flushed with good living. His eyes, the deep sloe-black of most Konaparians, were just a little sleepy-lidded, with a gleam of temper veiled behind. His complexion was clear and his voice was hearty and pleasant. He was a man's man who knew how to be liked by those under him. Chan liked him, and Chan wouldn't have trusted him as far as he could throw the *Warspear* off the surface of Jupiter.

Captain Alain, also observing the lusty ambition in the man, saw that he was the kind who never grabs with one hand, but uses both.

"What are your arms, Captain?" the Konaparian ruler was saying, and those sleepy eyes were registering caution at sight of a man as powerful and as obviously experienced in space war as the Cap.

Gan Alain grinned, a kind of respectful, now-you're-joking grin, and said: "Ah-ahh! We mercenaries have our little secrets. We have to be a wee bit ahead of the average military armament to stay alive, you know. I'll guarantee to best any ship my tonnage, and most of them twice that, if necessary."

Chan DuChaile snickered at the Cap's effrontery, here in the midst of a war-fleet of total strangers, and refraining from telling his armament or its range.

The Regent colored the slightest bit, but his face didn't move a muscle. "Now, by Satan, Captain, how can I direct your ship in battle if I don't know your range?"

"It won't be necessary to direct my ship in battle, Your Highness," answered the captain. "Employers invariably put mercenaries in the fore of every battle, since they do not have to pay dead men. My duties will consist only of guarding your person and your ship from surprise attack, let us say, by ambitious parties unknown who would stand to benefit by your demise. Agreed?"

FOR A LONG minute the Cap's eyes held the Regent's,

eye to eye in a subtle exchange, a kind of measuring of each other. The Regent, whose name was Gunnar Tor Branthak, pulled his beard thoughtfully, and his color went back to its normal ruddy hue.

"I do not expect any attacks by unnamed parties, but I fully understand your meaning. Those are your terms, and I accept them. Your pay will be regular battle pay equal to that received by my native supporters of equal rank. Naturally you will receive a share in the loot, which should amount to a fortune. But, you are aware I am not contracting to protect *you* against any resentment your lack of enterprise under fire might arouse?"

It was Captain Alain's turn to flush with repressed anger, and his big fist came up in a gesture that said more than any words. Just the same, he supplied the words to go with the fist. "If any man finds cause to reproach the *Warspear* for cowardly actions during battle, I will claim no share of any prize won by the forces of Konapar. The name of Captain Gan Alain should be warranty enough of the value of this ship to your project!"

"Agreed then!" the Regent snapped. "The *Warspear* will fight under my personal direction, and take orders from no other officers whatever." The 'visor went blank and Gan Alain turned and gave Chan a wink.

Chan grinned inwardly. What had happened was an example of the cool wits of his commander. The *Warspear* had jetted into an imperial war fleet staffed with jealous nobles and officers of royal blood, and contracted to guard the Regent from treachery from anyone of them. Chan would have bet that there were a dozen sub-potentates who were at this moment boiling violently around the collar and unable to do anything about it but sizzle. Who but the Cap would realize and take advantage of the fact that every ruler has his enemies, and that they would be looking for an opportunity such as might occur in battle to blast the Regent's ship by "mistake".

Gan Alain had learned by sad experience that a mercenary takes an unequal chance in battle beside allies, many of whom are relatives. They will send a hireling to his doom every time in preference to a brother or a cousin or a rich neighbor. The Tor's deal gave him a ship, which could have no ulterior motive, as the *Warspear's* crew stood to gain nothing unless the Tor remained alive.

ALL THIS time little Elvir sat silently in the control cabin perched on top of the file cabinet, her knees holding the chart book where the course to Konapar was scrawled out in red ink. She closed the big folder of charts and pushed it into the cabinet between her knees without getting down. Her eyes were half-shut, and the mate figured she was thinking about the women who ruled Phila and what was going to happen shortly to them. He chucked her under her pretty, round chin and asked: "Are you worried about the Amazons, chicken? We won't hurt them, if they behave themselves."

She shook her head, gave him a peculiar smile. Then she qualified the gesture with a confidential whisper the Cap couldn't hear. "I'm really thinking about the women, but it's because I'm worrying about what will become of Captain Alain when he gets mixed up with a city full of nothing but old women."

To Elvir, any woman over eighteen was old.

The inference behind her words tickled Chan so that he laughed. She grinned too, her eyes sparkling up at him, woman-wise in a child's face. It hit him suddenly. "Don't worry about the Cap where women are concerned. He can take 'em or leave 'em alone." He eyed her with wonder in his gaze. The scamp was actually jealous, and not with any childish jealousy, either.

She shook her curls again. "You don't know about the Priestesses. I do! I was to be a slave in the Temple of Myrmi-Atla, the glorious All-Mother. The other slaves talked about them all the time. They're not ordinary women; they're sorceresses."

The mate pooh-poohed the idea. "There's no such thing as sorcery, child. Not on Phira, anyway."

"You'll see," she predicted direly, knowingly with the all-wisdom of a child. "They'll wind the captain around their fingers. And I don't want to see it. I like him too much to see him made a fool of. If I was elder, I'd do something about it."

Chan wanted to say bluntly: "What?" but sight of her serious face made him think better of it. Instead he said: "Tell you what, Elvir; you and I can look ahead a little. We can plan to outfigure them. If some of the Matriarchs get under his skin, we'll fix them, eh?"

She put her child's hand in the mate's horny paw and shook. "It's a deal, Chan."

CHAPTER THREE

THE PHIRANS must have had plenty of warning of the attacking fleet, for their armada was sighted some four hours out of their solar system. Their ships were old, a style obsolete for half a century, which is a long time in the growth of galactic science. However, they had obviously been recently refitted and newly engined, for those blunt, clumsy power hogs were fairly splitting the ether when Konaparian telescopes identified them.

They split their forces right and left, which could be taken either for feminine thinking or stupidity, for no man would have divided his power that way. Tor Branthak took imme-diate advantage of the weakness and blasted his forces into the opening between and poured fission bombs and detonator rays right and left into the Phiran fleet. It looked to Chan as if the battle were ended before it had begun. The women had lost.

Gan Alain kept the *Warspear* right on the Regent's tail where he could see what was going on and be ready to repel attack as per agreement.

Then the Phirans, old and dilapidated as their fleet seemed, sprang a surprise. They had opened in the center just wide enough to get out of the way of a huge dark shape coming up from their rear. They had kept a screen of ships between it and the Konaparians or it would have been seen before. Now it was too late. Chan recognized her after a minute and sang out a warning.

"That's a Mixar ship, Cap! She carries potent stuff!"

Chan knew Mixar was on the outer rim of the Dires cluster, and that this ship must have been a year making the trip to Phira; thus her presence here must be due solely to chance: But that chance looked like disaster to the Konaparians. This thing was a super-dreadnought in size, and no one really knew what a Mixar ship packed in armament. The cult of Myrmi-Atla had originally come from the planets of the Regulus group, where the Mixar Amazons had kept out all intruders since the earliest days of space travel. When he said she was potent, Chan had understated the case. Tor Branthak's heart must have bounced in his boots when he saw her.

The big ship opened fire at once. A ray came out of her nose turret that must have been three feet wide at the orifice, and it broadened its bath. It struck the nearest of its enemies, a Konapar cruiser, then lanced swiftly right and left while Konaparian ships zoomed frantically right and left and up and down—any way to leave the vicinity of that dread, dark shape. The ships the ray had touched seemed unaffected as they drove straight on in their courses, through the Phiran fleet; but the fact that they did not fire a shot revealed the truth—they were manned by dead men.

Chan took a look at the visiscreen to see what the fleet was doing as a whole. The *Warspear* and the Regent's, big master-class cruiser were almost the only force now left in range of the Mixar threat, the rest of the valiant Konaparians rapidly vanishing to the rear. Space torpedoes were blossoming into fire against the Mixar hull, but the men who had fired them had left the scene.

The torpedoes didn't seem to effect her armor. She boomed on inexorably nearer the Regent's ship, and it struck Gan Alain that the Regent was only waiting to see what his new employee could do about it—which was silly, as the Mixar was at least ten times the *Warspear's* size. Actually, the Regent was probably stunned with surprise, and had unconsciously looked to his newest ally for a possible salvation of the situation.

The Cap had a tight grin on his grim face, and Chan watched him pull the graviton-sphere hatch lever, watched the glowing sphere of charged metal drift out into space. Gan Alain was revealing one of his special weapons, and probably with it, its range. Perhaps the Regent would be surprised in a disagreeable as well as a pleasant way.

GAN FLICKED a repulsor ray against the sphere, and it moved sluggishly off toward the Mixar ship. Then the Cap spun the *Warspear* end-for-end and gave the rear jets to the deadly sphere. The *Warspear* went away fast, but the rough iron sphere of red hot metal bobbed equally fast, though more clumsily, on its way toward the big stranger, looking about as harmless as a hunk of asteroid rock.

The maneuver was probably as incomprehensible to the Mixars as it was to the Regent, who turned tail too, and fled after the *Warspear*. The graviton sphere is a device that is unknown in the Dires system. The *Warspear* had gone far to pick that up.

The sphere went humping along toward the enemy, who seemed to watch it contemptuously. They swerved the Mixar gently aside to avoid it, no more than necessary. The sphere swerved too, and now picked up speed. The Mixar took alarm then and, like the *Warspear*, spun around and gave it their rear jets.

What they didn't know was that the sphere was carrying a motor generator creating gravitons, which was fueled by a fission metal, which was also its warhead. It manufactured gravitons so fast that its artificial gravity was by now nearly equal to a big planet like Phira, and it was so close that all the blasts in the Mixar fuel tanks couldn't drive it away. They were trying to escape a thing that nothing ever escaped, unless, like Cap, they got away before the generator really got up speed. Since the sphere had no genuine inertia or mass of its own, its artificial gravity drew it toward any object inexorably, in spite of all attempts to escape.

The jets had no effect upon the sphere, for it wasn't the same chunk of iron it had been when the *Warspear's* jets started it on its way. Now it was a vast contact bomb, homing on the Mixar ship, and its graviton generators were stepping up more revolutions by the second.

The only effective defense against the thing now was to bomb or torpedo it so that it wasted its explosive force in space, but its size was so small that this was a virtual impossibility in the short time remaining. The Mixar had made the mistake of trying to blast it away with its jets, as it had seen the *Warspear* do.

The explosion blew a hole in the Mixar's rear into which the *Warspear* could have driven and parked, with room for a theater besides.

The Mixar dreadnought lost way, drifted slowly in a circle, her jets guttering as she tried vainly to get going again. Then she blew up, giving off a glare of light like a little star as her fuel fissioned.

The disaster took the heart out of Phira and put it back into the Konaparian fleet. The invaders appeared again from out of the blue yonder. The Phirans smashed into them, fighting heroically, but with no apparent tactic but desperation. They were well weaponed, but outnumbered. With better tactics, they might have counted heavily, but it was evident they had based their hopes on the big ship from the neighboring solar system, and that it had contained their tactical brains, too.

The Cap grinned as he eased his big body from the control seat and motioned Chan to replace him. "It looks as if the Matriarchs are going to have to take masculine orders for awhile," he said to Chan, but the mate didn't smile.

"I don't like it, Captain," said Chan. "What have you got against the Phiran females you should knock their pins out for Konapar? How do you know it wouldn't have paid better to fight for the women, as it is natural for a man to do?"

Gan frowned, shook his head. "You'll find out, DuChaile. Wait until you understand the Matriarchs; then you'll agree."

The Phirans fled, reformed, tried to meet Konapar again on the edge of their solar system. But it was no good. They lost two to one in a brief, raging encounter. They fled again, a fifth of the fleet that had come out to meet the invaders. The rest drifted, hulls riddled, along the route they had so recently covered.

It was the only resistance to the invasion. When a scout party jetted down over Alid, a white flag of surrender floated over the spire of the Temple of Myrmi-Atla—and the Temple of Alid rules all Phira.

CHAPTER FOUR

CELYS, high priestess of Myrmi-Atla, stood peering from the ornate leaded panes of her sanctum in the temple. She watched the orange sky where one by one the great warships of Konapar loomed out of the flaming horizon, grew huger, settled to a landing on the plateau above the valley where the Holy City stretched along the high, curving banks of the sacred river Kroon.

There were tears in the lovely emerald-flecked gold eyes of the priestess. Her long lashes were wet, and her slender hands upon the black and gold of the drapes trembled with anger. She knew quite well why Gunnar Tor Branthak had broken treaty with Phira. It was not for gold, not for loot, not for power. What the Tor wanted was *the secret!*

Beside the window the dark stones slid silently aside, revealing an opening and a passage within the seemingly solid wall. In the darkness a tall, pale figure moved like a cold flame, silent as a ghost. Celys turned as the figure reached out and touched her shoulder. The two stood with eyes fixed upon each other, then, as if moved by identical emotion, joined in close embrace. The one who had entered from the wall murmured: "It had been so very long, dear. The Mother has sent me to replace you. You are to return to Avalaon. She needs to take council in this crisis, and you should be there."

Celys released herself from the arms of the newcomer. As they turned about each other, the illusion of one slipping into the place of the other was magically perfect. Anyone watching would have sworn some mystery of identity was here, for the two women seemed to have changed places, yet Celys still stood by the window. One glided into the wall, which returned to its seeming solidity, and the other moved into the identical posture in which Celys had stood, peering through the lifted drapes over the conquered city. And there was no change in her. It was Celys, high priestess of Myrmi-Atla, the supreme power over all the planet Phira until today.

Celys turned from the window, letting the dark drape fall and shut out the hated sight of the conquerors. She stood, a pale flame in the temple gloom, a lance of green in her diaphanous robe—the green that symbolized the lifeblood of the All-Mother—topped by the ruddy hue of her rich red-gold hair, curled and coifed high, bound in a net of emeralds. She stood, weeping silently, her face stiff from the effort to keep from sobbing aloud.

Across the polished stone paving of the temple chamber came a swiftly running white-robed figure, one of the acolytes, a girl of perhaps fourteen. She swept to a half-salaam before Celys, then clasped her about the waist, her voice choked: "Dear Mistress, I know how your heart twists in pain. But let us go—the Empress in Mixar offers asylum. The ship waits, why will you not go to safety? We do not matter, but *you* bear the very torch of the true religion in your breast. You must save it, to light the fire where it will not be snuffed out again."

Celys put her hand on the girl's head and raised her face. "No, little one, I may not shame the Mother by running away. I, before all others, must face the conqueror without fear."

The girl clung to her silently for a moment, then as in an afterthought, said: "There is a little messenger come to you, a tiny wisp of a girl. She says she comes from an enemy ship and bears a secret message. I thought she lied, or was mad, for it hardly makes sense."

"Send her to me," said Celys.

LITTLE Elvir stood before Celys, somewhat abashed by her regal beauty and the sadness in her face. But her pretty chin squared with determination, and her child's heart beat madly, her mind spinning with plans.

She began: "I slipped away when no one was looking, to see for myself the city of Amazons, where women rule men, and men are but servants."

Celys' eyes went chill, and she half turned away. "If that is all the child wants, take her and put her outside the temple gates."

Eloi, the acolyte who had shown her into the sanctum, took Elvir firmly by the arm, but the little slave girl twisted free and darted behind the tall form of Celys.

"That isn't all. I bear an important message that Captain Gan Alain would trust to no one but me."

"What is the message, sparrow?" asked Celys coldly, withdrawing slightly from the somewhat grimy hand that clutched her immaculate skirts.

"Not Gan Alain, the pirate?" queried Eloi, pausing in her circling attempt to catch the quick little child.

Elvir shrieked at her, horrified at her words. "He's *not* a pirate! He's a privateer, and the bravest fighting man in all space."

"The difference is found only in the spelling of the word," commented Celys, smiling in spite of herself at the loyalty on the pert face.

Eloi's eyes caught those of Celys, both of them realizing that here might be some kind of a lever, some tiny opening in the conqueror's armor. Gan Alain was a mercenary, mercenaries can be bought, and here was contact with one in the pay of the enemy. Celys bent, then, her eyes searching the child's face for character, to know whether her words would be lies or not.

"Tell me quickly, child. Did your master send you, and is he in the employ of Tor Branthak?"

"That he did, and that he is. He wants you Amazon women to hide yourselves, to have no contact with the enemy in any way. Otherwise a terrible fate will befall you."

Celys laughed, suddenly perceiving the real mind behind the message. "And did your master truly say those words, little sparrow, or did you yourself get them from some storybook?"

But now, Eloi, who had again caught hold of Elvir's slender wrist, suddenly raised it so that Celys could see and cried out: "She has the sign of the Mother upon her forearm! She is one of our own temple slaves!"

Celys looked startled, bent and peered at the little blue scroll and enclosed symbol of Myrmi-Atla upon Elvir's arm.

"Where did you come from, imp? And what do you want? Answer truly, or I'll have you thrashed until you tell the truth!"

Elvir had been whipped before. Tears gathered in her eyes, and at last she blurted out: "I only wanted Captain Gan to stay away from the Amazons…and I didn't know what else to do."

Celys' further questions proved of no help. Her origin remained a mystery, except that it was obvious that the ship from which the Cap had taken her was one bought and paid for by a Phiran buyer, at which time Elvir had received the indelible tattoo of ownership. Celys had her sent to the slaves' quarters and proceeded to forget about her. Tor Branthak would demand audience within the hour and she must make ready. She had no time for a silly child. As for Tor Branthak, she could not imagine what she should be ready for, except that it would not be pleasant.

CHAPTER FIVE

ON THE great plateau above the city—where the fleet lay while the troops disembarked, formed ranks, marched down the steep highway into the city—a council of war was being held. In the salon of Tor Branthak's flagship officers stood at attention as the bearded Regent gave final orders for the occupation of Alid. One by one the officers saluted, wheeled, left on the double to join the waiting troops.

When the room was quite empty, Gan Alain found himself alone, facing the quizzical smile of the Regent. For a long moment the silence held as the two big men measured each other, then the Regent gave a booming laugh and reached out with a big hand to shake the Captain's. Gan smiled. The ruler was hard to resist. He had a way with men and it was evident that his officers admired him.

"I suppose, Captain, that you are wondering just where you fit in now that the nut is cracked? Whether you come out catbird or get some of the meat? To tell you the truth, to get the most out of you, I've got to offer you the most. Sit down."

The furnishings of the salon were screwed fast to the floor plates, and the only place to sit near at hand was the top of an ornate desk. Alain sat, swinging one booted leg from the edge. The Regent crossed behind it, swung open a door in the back, handed a tall flagon of blue liquor and two glasses to the Cap. Gan set the glasses down, and the Regent sat in the chair behind the desk. Gan filled the glasses raised one to eye level, grinned as he toasted: "To Myrmi-Atla and her daughters, the priestesses of Sacred Alid. May they live...*long*."

Gan waited, his eyes on the suddenly wary eyes of Tor Branthak. Slowly the ruler picked up his glass and, as Gan touched his own to his lips, tossed the liquor down his throat with a quick motion and set the glass down hard as if he had made a decision.

"I was going to tell you anyway, Captain, but since you know, it makes it simpler. It's not generally known, you realize?"

Valigurđy

Gan's voice was hard and even, without a shade of emotion. "On the contrary, it's well known."

"My officers do *not* know! As far I have been able to learn, I'm the only man in all the forces of Konapar who does know for a certainty what treasure these women hold in secret. For to whom could a man trust a secret so valuable?"

Gan Alain's voice remained even and calm as he echoed: "To whom trust—immortality?"

"My spies stole the record books from the temple some time ago. Those records reach back many centuries, Captain Alain. In those records are many deaths, and every death is male! Yet the entire organization of this religion of theirs is

The odor of seared flesh permeated the room, and the man's horrible screams resounded

dominated, staffed—by women! It's impossible!"

Gan's voice echoed the Regent's once more: "Impossible but true, Your Highness. Quite true. And not the secret you think. I've heard it in rumor often. Once I had it by word of mouth from one who claimed to know. They *don't* die, these women!"

The Regent's voice took on a note of awe, of puzzlement, and ended in an angry exclamation: "They live on and on! But how? Man, how?"

Alain shrugged, his face expressionless.

The Regent clenched a big fist, struck it on the table. "We're *men*, Captain. They are women who deny this thing to any man, deny it to any but members of their sacrosanct religious organization. We've got to wring it out of them some way. *Any* way. I can't go after it openly—my followers would think me mad to believe such an impossible story. But you and I, knowing, having them in our hands, under our absolute power—it will be strange if we can't get the truth out of them, or out of at least *one* of them!"

GAN STOOD up, leaned over the desk to bring his face on a level with Tor Branthak's. "Give me a free hand, Tor Branthak! Back my play with your authority. Put my men in charge of the main temple and the priestesses. When I get the secret, then we open it up, make it known to all, and your conquest will be justified in all men's eyes and you will become a savior, a champion who fights for all men against an ugly, secretive monopoly—of life itself! We'll have proof…"

"*If* we tell them, Captain. It's a problem unique to my experience. A lot depends on the nature of the secret. Is it a drug, a medicine, a ray, or is it some damned impossible abracadabra of their religion, something we couldn't give away if we wanted to? For that matter, why tell anyone if we do find it?"

"We'll find it! What do you think I threw in with you for? What you do with it after we find it is entirely up to you, Tor Branthak. I'll know too, and I'll not deny such a thing to my friends. I've small respect for Myrmi-Atla if she teaches her worshippers to keep such a secret from all mankind. Or for her priestesses! They'll find my hand heavy enough, never fear."

Gan Alain straightened, his eyes still holding the dark, hot eyes of Tor Branthak. "Just one more thing, Your Highness. I've a reputation for square dealing. I've also a reputation for getting even. This thing is quite a prize, and a terrible temptation. I'll go along with you as long as I get aboveboard treatment. But *don't*, Tor Branthak, deal off the bottom of the deck. Don't even consider it!"

"You threaten me, Captain?"

For an instant there flashed between the two men a kind of still, terrible lightning; a leashed and fearful power of strange and threatening nature. That lightning came from the glance of Gan Alain's eyes upon Tor Branthak's, a piercing into him of personal power, so that for an instant the Regent's fingers shook on the stem of his glass. As Gan turned away, strode for the door, Tor Branthak poured the glass full again, sipped it slowly, his eyes brooding upon the door through which Gan's broad back disappeared. At last the ruler set his drink down with a hand that was steady again, and his full, sensuous lips twisted in a smile of pure delight—delight tinged with sinister exultation. It was the kind of smile a breaker of horses gives who has bought a seemingly average mount of good appearance, only to find, when astride it, a creature filled with wild, unbounded vitality—a horse hard to break, but infinitely valuable once broken. Tor Branthak spoke aloud to the empty room—and his words were a cold, heavy music ringing in the silence:

"Now that was a mistake, my captain, to show me *that* in you!"

CHAPTER SIX

THE ANCIENT Temple of Myrmi-Atla was a vast pile, very old and many times rebuilt and enlarged. There were chambers within chambers, passages in the walls unknown even to the present occupants, and secret chambers known only to the inner circle.

Within one of these secret chambers stood now at attention a hundred young, strong women—warrior women bearing weapon harnesses as if the leather grew upon them. Their eyes were fixed upon a flaming-haired beauty who stood before their ranks with hands outstretched in benediction.

"You go, war maidens, not in fear or in flight, but only to make ready the way for your return. Our Mother needs time to meet this new threat to the Matriarchy; but the rule of women will not perish from Phira. In every other world known to mankind, the male is dominant, save on Mixar. But it is here, and here alone, where woman fills her proper place in life. Here alone is woman not a downtrodden chattel, not a plaything, not a decoration or a mere bearer of children; but the end and aim of all of the race's existence. You go to Alavaon, not to hide, but to study our conqueror from far-off, and to learn his weaknesses; and when he has forgotten the warrior-women of Myrmi-Atla, we will strike. When all thoughts of peril from our ancient power has vanished from his mind—we will strike, and once again the All-Mother will rule in the same old way. Go, my sisters; go with love and without shame. Shame will come only when you forget our purpose and become again but fireside kittens purring at the feet of the dominant male."

Her words rang with a sincere and ardent determination. On the faces of all the handsome war-maidens the same purpose lived and shone from their eyes, glanced from the hardened muscles of their rosy jaws, breathed with each lift of lovely, proudly swelling young breasts—made for love yet hardened by teaching and encompassing steel to the taste for war and struggle. Red as new-shed blood were their uniforms, slim, graceful legs clad in sleek, shining plasticord, weapon belt, with dagger and needle-gun holster hugging each graceful hip, torso and fair breasts covered with the brilliance of ray-proof flex-steel, shoulders bearing proudly the folded glide-wings of the air-soldier, back wearing the small triple cylinders of the standard atomic jet drive for all glide-wings, strong and graceful arms ringed about with the deadly lightning rings, that Terran-forbidden device of prisoned electrons released only by the ray of the needle gun on their hips.

They were as well equipped, as well trained in appearance, as deadly a group of fighting humans as could be found in the entire galaxy. But for them to fight now, with the heavy weaponed ships of Tor Branthak and his horde of Konaparians commanding the plateau overlooking the city - with their own fleet almost destroyed—was out of the question. So they saluted, filed into the passage and down to the hidden tunnel, which would conduct them from the city. These were the temple guard, and from all the city that day similar groups of warrior women had been stealing away by secret ways to a rendezvous in hidden Avalaon.

Avalaon had served them in historic times more than once as a reservoir of hidden strength in similar crises. For the rule of women in Phira had been challenged by the war fleets of a dozen powers in times past, powers and empires now passed away and forgotten. But the rule of Myrmi-Atla and her warrior maids, of her teacher-priestesses, had survived.

After their going, the temple lay empty and waiting. There were present only the young acolytes, a few of the superior priestesses, and Celys, the present high priestess, to await the advent of the conqueror and to render him homage.

THE ACOLYTES of Myrmi-Atla were gathered in the great main chamber of worship, before a heroic stone figure of the All-Mother, where Celys led them in singing hymns. They were awaiting their fate, and the furtive glances the young girls threw at the wide doorways for the first glimpse of the inrush of the male conquerors were of two kinds. For their contacts with men of any kind had been nonexistent, and though they had been taught to fear all men of teachings other than Myrmi-Atla's, still nature herself made their young hearts beat not only with fear but also with anticipation. In the case of Celys, however, the occasional glance she allowed herself would have betrayed her very real emotions to no one.

The expected rape of the temple seemed to have been delayed. The hymns went on and on, and when at last they heard the booted feet ringing upon the sacred paves of the dedicated halls, and raised their voices in even more fervent appeals to the All-Mother, the tramping feet came to a stamping halt some distance from the main doorway.

A single pair of feet moved close now, after a ringing command, and paused quite reverently at the very center of the arched opening. Just as all men of Phira who are devout must remain without any chamber which contains an image of the All-Mother enshrined, the booted conqueror remained.

Celys, her face puzzled at this courteous behavior from the enemy, waved a hand to Eloi, who took her place at the altar. Then Celys moved on silent, graceful feet to meet her fate.

There was a lone man waiting at the door. He was big, scarred, hard, muscular. He was handsome enough, she noted, his mane of hair like curled golden wires in the lamp light. His face was lined with creases of laughter about the mouth, deep crinkles about the corners of the eyes, fierce lines of anger and effort now relaxed. The observing eye of Celys caught them all. His wide cheeks and heavy jaw were bronzed deeply, and his costume, she thought, was far too swashbuckling an assembly of colors and metals to be seemly for any but a blood-dyed pirate. On each thigh swung a hand weapon of a design Celys did not recognize. Had she known what those weapons had done and could do, it is possible she would have dropped in a faint before him.

Celys put him down as a man impatient of all restraint, a ruthless, domineering rogue who used his looks and laughter only to disarm unsuspecting womankind. She was sure the straight-seeming honesty of his eyes was only a guise to outwit other rogues less clever than he.

Celys stood just inside the white line that marked the border where no male foot might treat without eternal damnation from the All-Mother, eyeing this monster out of space with all the chill she could muster against his smiling nonchalance. Gan waited, and she waited, each for the other to speak first. Celys lost the struggle.

She shook her head impatiently, stamped her slim, sandaled foot. "What do you want? Who are you? Why are you here?"

Gan did not answer at once, but stood eyeing her and allowing an expression of astonishment to spread slowly across his features. At last he said, with exaggerated respect: "I had expected a much older woman, Mother Celys! How old are you, anyway? Not a day over twenty-five, by appearance."

A FLUSH of embarrassment and anger swept upward from Celys' white neck, and her tongue seemed to stumble as she snapped: "My age is my business. It is also my business to know what you are doing in the temple at this hour of the evening? No male visitors are allowed except between the hours of three and four in the afternoon."

The smile left Gan Alain's face. His voice became hard and smooth as glass. "My lady, you know very well why I am here. This city has fallen into the hands of the Regent of Konapar. To ensure the safety of your priestesses and the rest of your hennery, he has sent me, whom he considers honorable, to protect you from the looting and rapine of conquest. If you expect me to carry out this assignment efficiently, you had better come down off your horse and cooperate. I have already posted my men at the entrances to this warren of misguided female bigots. It would be better if you didn't mistake where the power rests from now on."

Celys' eyes searched the intruder's strong and bronzed

face for an instant, then she bowed her head for a long minute in silent prayer, her lips moving as she asked the All-Mother for guidance. But Gan moved his feet impatiently.

"It would be best if you showed me the place completely. It could well be that I have overlooked the entries and exits which most need guards. No one is to leave without my personal permission, Mother. Understand?"

As Celys raised her head from prayer, she moved silently out before him, expecting to precede him. But he swung into step beside her, and she started at the sound of a score of feet swinging into step behind them. She gave him a glance of pure irritation, but his handsome face remained inscrutable; mockingly so, she decided. She turned her eyes from him with difficulty. There was something indescribably fascinating in the man's presence, a power and dignity she could not recall having remarked in any other man. Mentally she gave herself a kick at the incongruity of finding power and dignity in the gaudy garb of a pirate.

Celys was not familiar with the rich worlds of space traffic, the brawling, spawning ports of the spaceways. She could not know that Gan's worn corselet of dull gold leather, gemmed with synthetic rubies, his close-fitting breeches of black plasticord with gold piping, the black weapon belt and silver-handled explosive pellet guns made up a costume that in many places would have been considered plain to the point of shabbiness.

But in one way Celys was right. No clothing could conceal the rich wealth of vitality, the vaulting spirit, the leashed physical strength of the man. To Celys' eyes, the swell and ripple of muscles upon his bare arms, where the light glinted from little golden hairs everywhere, was positively vulgar. This barbarian, she muttered angrily to herself, had now all power over the temple, it seemed!

"Did you say something, Mother?" asked Alain, hiding a

smile at her reaction to the way he used the word "mother".

Celys stilled her angry thoughts with a practiced facility and flashed him the first smile he had seen upon her face. "Why do you keep calling me 'mother'? Certainly you have lived longer than I."

"On my home planet," answered Gan easily, "we call all women of religious orders 'mother'. Does the word irk you?"

"Oh, no." And Celys gave her head a toss of impatience. "Not at all, Father."

Gan gave his chin a thoughtful massage with his palm. If she was intending to hide what Tor Branthak wanted, she had made a good start. It surely *seemed* that she considered herself younger than he. But then again, the truth might be even more irritating, if she were indeed a creature who had lived several lifetimes in some strange renewal of youth. This was going to take some sharp work, he foresaw.

THE TEMPLE was vast, and after two hours of steady pacing up and down stairs and halls, of peering into chambers filled with accumulations of centuries of female living, Gan was ready to call a halt.

"Before heaven, dear lady," he swore, "let us collect your charges into one corner of this compost heap and post our guards so that we may get some sleep. I've been through a hard day, if you have not."

Celys did not even pause in her long, lithe striding. Her voice was subtly mocking. "I had thought to find our conquerors spending the first night in celebration, in drinking and lewd wallowing with their captive women. Yet here is a great, brawny hero crying for bed like a sleepy boy. For shame!"

Gan was really tired, and her attitude was getting under his skin. He growled in utter irritation. "It might behoove your petty mightiness to keep a civil tongue, at least until this brawl really settles down. Anything can happen, including those things you have mentioned. They *will* happen if I don't guard you!"

In sudden meekness, Celys turned about and they returned to the main chamber, where the assembled female followers of the mysterious All-Mother still sang in weary voices.

Gan asked: "Isn't there any place where you study; any classrooms, laboratories, workshops where you teach crafts? Is there nothing but sleeping and praying rooms in the whole place?"

Celys' voice seemed to catch in her throat as she said: "Not...not in the holy temple, Captain. In the schools, which lie without the temple walls, and in other places, are such things taught. Here we teach the Word of the All-Mother only."

"Hmmph!" Gan grunted, and turning on his heel, left her, calling over his shoulder, "Goodnight, Mother."

He was a little surprised that she returned only silence.

CHAPTER SEVEN

WITH THE morning sun Tor Branthak came, at the head of two-score gorgeously uniformed personal guards, to "check the temple for resistance". He greeted Celys where she waited at the center of the great doorway into the shrine of the All-Mother. The Regent knew very well that no male was allowed to cross the white line upon pain of Myrmi-Atla's infinite anger. So he strode across and, into the very center of the clustered young priestesses, smilingly eyeing them right and left as if measuring them for girdles. Celys pursued him with horrified face, catching up with him as he turned in wonder that no common soldier of his guard had followed him into the ancient shrine.

"It is forbidden! You intrude!" Celys was crying out, over

and over, as if the words were a ritual. Her repeated cry at last angered the Regent.

"Young woman, it is the custom to address me as 'Your Majesty', as I am the virtual emperor of all the might of Konapar, and lately of Phira also. But of course, you being a woman, you could not be expected to recognize any authority but your own willfulness. Or can you?"

Celys stood frozen, shock overcoming her at meeting the one being she had most dreaded to meet since the first hostilities. Tor Branthak went on speaking.

"Well, well, my charming priestess, had I known there were such attractive morsels of femininity here, I should have arrived much sooner. Somehow I had expected the Matriarch's intimates to be much older and much uglier than you. Now, dear lady, could you direct me to the creature in charge of this antiquated pile of obsolete masonry?"

Celys' shock was turning into anger at his disrespect for all things Phiran and she found herself unable to answer. The Regent prodded her. "Come, come—someone looks after all these god-addled female wits, do they not? Where would I find such a one, or have her tasks overcome her mind, too?"

Celys drew herself up, anger and pride and humiliation all mingled in her voice. "I am known as the Supreme Matriarch, Your Majesty. You must forgive my not knowing who you were. I had no warning you would arrive at this time."

The Regent snorted. "You have had warning enough, woman. When the fleet settled down over Alid yesterday, you might know the temple would be visited today. But, you look so very young for such a high position. Tell me, what is your age?"

Celys remained silent, smiling aloofly, as if she had not heard his question. The Regent eyed her, his black eyes snapping with suppressed anger, his fingers clamped on the hilt of his decorative sword at his waist.

"You must know, if you are a Supreme Matriarch, something of the legend of longevity that is commonly related about you. In the records of Phiran events, there has been a certain Celys in office for some two hundred years. I want to know if you are that woman, or some other?"

Celys' voice was low and calm now, and her eyes veiled as if she recited words from memory. "My name is Celys, it is true, but that is a ritual name. All Supreme Matriarchs take the name of Celys. It is but custom. I have not been in office for so very long."

The Regent pushed his face forward almost into hers. "*Just* how long, and what is your real name? Answer me! You were the Supreme Matriarch forty years ago; I have that from several eyewitnesses who recognized you. I want to know what is the secret of your perpetual youth?"

"There is no secret, your Highness, believe me. We of Phira come of a long-lived stock. There are, the shorter-lived breeds scattered among us, so that our life spans vary from the so-called norm to three and four times the normal. That is all of the secret, and it will do no good to question me, for I can tell you no more than the truth."

GAN ALAIN, who had been awakened by his orderly, hurried up, buckling his belt, tugging his leather corselet straight. He hesitated at the forbidden white line, then grinned and strode across as the assembled young virgins glared at this repeated desecration. Gan's words were still slow with sleep.

"How went affairs in the city overnight, Commander?"

The Tor turned from his intent regard of the Matriarch's masklike white, face and smiled broadly at Gan. His answer came with a chuckle: "The householders of Alid put up a spirited resistance, Captain, but aside from several flurries of armed resistance, all went well. The women resented our masculinity vigorously, and they repeatedly attempted to put our warriors in their place—namely out of doors. But all in all, love won, and the militancy of the female population seems much abated today."

Gan grinned, realizing that it must have been quite a night for all concerned, and looking at Celys' white and furious face, at her jaws clamped on the furious rhetoric she would like to have used, he burst out laughing.

"That's capital news, Your Highness. It would have been too bad to have been forced to fight. The women of Phira are too pretty to kill. And the men do not fight, it seems."

Tor Branthak turned back to the Matriarch. "You say there is no secret? I would like more in that vein."

Celys composed herself with an effort, forcing her words into a semblance of civility. "It is just that you are unacquainted with the teachings of the All-Mother. Everyone who worships in our shrines; all over Phira and over some ten other planets, knows that the principle figures of the Matriarchate are supposed to be immortal. Few believe it, accepting it only as a pleasant fiction, a survival from a more ignorant time. As I have told you, the truth is we come of long-lived blood lines, and our offices are hereditary."

The Regent snorted again, his eyes cold now, his face no longer smiling, but with a black look like a gathering storm: "So it is a pleasant fiction? As it happens, my dear no-longer Supreme Matriarch, I have the records of the Matriarchy in my possession. Those worn books give rather intimate details of the inner workings of your fantastically powerful organization, reaching back some eight centuries. I know the truth, Celys. Why do you think I risked my life, my position and the honor of the Empire of Konapar in this war? I want that information!"

Celys' sudden laugh was superb acting. It was scornful of the Regent's ignorance and credulity. It rang with merriment at the impossibly devastating results of one man's simple-minded belief in the impossible. It rang all through the gamut of ridicule, and as she laughed, the Regent's face paled, his eyes grew stormy and filled with a terrible anger, his ruddy cheeks sagged into murderous lines.

Celys, glancing into his eyes, paled suddenly and her laugh choked in her throat. She put out a hand as if to hold back the death she saw in his face. Her words were hurried and frightened.

"Of course the fiction is kept upon the books, Your Highness. Our people believe in their goddess and her in-finite powers. They believe in us, her immortal representatives. But surely a worldly man like you, who know the religions of a dozen sun-systems, must understand such anachronisms in all mysticism? It is an ancient religion, this worship of the All-Mother, surviving from a dark past, kept up because of the simple natures of our more lowly supporters. Surely you can't believe…"

GAN ALAIN looked at her in open admiration. She was gambling her life upon her ability to lie, and doing a superb job—or else he was a fool, and the Regent a bigger one. Gan rubbed his chin, bristly with the early-rising kinks that only a brush would remove, and eyed the Tor quizzically.

Tor Branthak's eyes narrowed. He studied the woman's pale, exquisite countenance for a long half-minute. Then he growled: "You will submit proofs of the deaths of your predecessors, the dates, and show my men their graves. And you will do the same for every other supposedly immortal member of your female conspiracy against the natural dominance of mankind over womankind. That means I want proof of births and dates and no trumped-up forged papers will serve. You'll either prove what you have just said, and that soon, my yellow-eyed beauty, or I'll have the truth out of you with hot pincers. No woman can sport two hundred years as if they were but twenty-five and keep the method secret from all other human beings—not while Tor Branthak has a will and a way. Now get out of my sight, before I order worse to happen to you."

The Tor's black eyes burned into hers with an intensity that left her no doubt as to his sincerity. She put a hand to her face, and seemed about to falter, her knees bending with the effect of his anger upon her, then she turned slowly and moved away, weaving slightly with a sudden weakness. The hearts of both men went out to her, then they caught each other's eyes and the signs of sympathy upon each face, and suddenly both burst out laughing at allowing a woman's pretense of weakness to disarm them.

"A damned fine actress," murmured the Regent.

"A very experienced one, at the least, Tor Branthak," muttered Gan Alain in reply. "But are we mere mortals strong enough to put our threats into force? Will she not cozen you some way into believing that it takes no special equipment to outlive others until you tire of life? Could you actually put a hot iron to that lovely flesh?"

Tor Branthak's face grew dark again, and the sympathy disappeared. "I can and I will, Captain! But first you will try every other method that may occur to you, for I must confess I admire the woman too much to want to kill her. But know the truth we shall before too long, and you can place your money on that."

Then the Regent spun on his heel and left, his boots ringing metallically on the stone pave, the virgin priestesses watching him go with horror in their soft young eyes.

Gan moved off in the wake of the vanishing figure of Celys, determined to spend as much time as possible with her, and to leave no stone unturned that might save her from a position that might actually be as she said—a mere relic from the dark past, an ancient artifice that was kept alive to fill the coffers of the temple.

Gan caught up with her where she stood alone in a corridor, leaning with one hand against the wall as if she had no strength to go further. It was in fact the first time in her life that she had been face to face with the threat of torture; and as she looked up from her reverie to find the scarred, bronzed visage of Gan Alain beside her, the reality of the horror that might be visited upon her found ample substantiation in his grim eyes. For Gan felt that if these women *did* conceal such a secret behind the facade of religious mummery, no fate was too evil for them.

NEITHER of them spoke, but they measured each other with intent eyes, looking for the hidden things behind, and finding in each other much of deep interest and attraction. The silence and the deep regard became embarrassing as there slowly flamed between them the inevitable fascination of vitality, which each possessed in so great a measure. Gan was looking for some slight evidence of a continued effort toward masquerade, toward the false drama he felt she knew could be her only defense. And he found that evidence, for he knew enough of women to know that the next card she would play would be her sex.

She came to him, as if drawn irresistibly, and she did it perfectly, her hair a pale glory about her glowing, brilliant eyes in the dimness, her body soft and warm beneath the soft robe of diaphanous green, her eyes grown heavy and sweet as if with sleep. His arms went about her, and their lips halted but inches from the other's, parted and anticipating the thrill to come, hers seemingly heavy with unspoken questions that could be answered in but one way.

Then Gan crushed her to him and drank deep of her scarlet mouth. Her, hands pressed him back ineffectually, then beat upon his chest, then suddenly relaxed and she became a limp weight in his arms. He released her, but she sagged downward and would have fallen had he not embraced her again. It was not until the weight in his arms told him that he had forgotten his strength and nearly crushed her that he felt remorse, and even then he was not sure but that it was only more acting. It was the logical next move, to play the part of an innocent virgin who faints at a kiss...but then these people of Phira could not have the strength that was his, their planet being but a third the weight of his own birthplace.

Long minutes later she raised her head and opened her eyes on his. She sighed. "Your arms are like steel bands. You can't be human!"

Gan was convinced. It had been an honest kiss, and his strength had caused unconsciousness. He determined to act as she would have expected had she been successful in deceiving him. He murmured: "I've been wanting to do that since I first saw you. Looking so sad and frightened, you were irresistible. Forgive me."

She released herself and her round, lovely arms raised, straightened her hair, the while she kept her evil eyes on his, soberly measuring him still again.

Just then a tiny form came racing up the corridor, flung itself against Gan bodily, embracing him, sobbing in unashamed delight. "Oh Captain Gan, they kept me locked up. I couldn't get back to you. Don't let them whip me again."

IT WAS little Elvir, dressed now in the simple yellow tunic of the temple slaves, which left her pretty legs exposed to the thighs, but covered the rest of her very modestly. Gan dropped an amazed hand to her curls, then, as astonishment over her sudden appearance abated, her words soaked into his somewhat bemused mind. He started in anger.

"And have you been whipped, little one?" he asked, his voice taking on the undertones of the angry bellow of which his crew lived in dread. "Tell me who did it, and why?"

Elvir, seeing the telltale flushed cheeks and heavy eyes of Celys, suddenly remembered her original errand into the temple, and her wits began to whir in double time.

"They wouldn't believe that I'm off the *Warspear*, and they shut me up with their slaves. Yesterday they whipped me for lying to them. I hate the priestesses, and I hate their old temple and the whole mess of lies they tell, too. *I* didn't lie; *they* did!"

Alain looked at Celys, wrath gathering in his eyes. "Was it you had Elvir whipped, dear lady?"

Celys, feeling that every possible avenue of reasonable relationships with these conquerors was inexorably closing before her, only saw one more obstacle arising in this silly child's words. Her neck stiffened, her eyes flashed.

"She bears the temple mark on her arm. So far as I am concerned, she belongs to Myrmi-Atla, and may be whipped if the priestesses desire."

"She happens to be my personal property," scowled Gan. "You will henceforth allow her the liberty of the temple and of the city. Do you understand, or must there be more words about the matter?"

Celys nodded slowly, not trusting herself to speak, but her eyes upon little Elvir's were pale as ice. She had had no idea it could be so terribly difficult to be in a subordinate position. Little things mattered so, suddenly. This was going to take masterly control, infinite tact and patience—and she had so little experience in the use of either.

Feeling that her days of liberty were numbered, she

became suddenly frightened and whirled and took flight from this terrible bronzed man of space, hastening down the interminable corridor with undignified strides. Gan watched her go, then strode off to check his guards and to search the temple and the nearby "schools" for more concrete evidence of the Matriarch's secret pursuits. At his heels tripped Elvir, her heart full of glee that Gan and the "old" chieftainess of the stuck-up priestesses weren't hitting it off.

CHAPTER EIGHT

DAYS LATER, with the Regent increasingly impatient, Gan's search led him into the subterranean maze of passages beneath the ancient temple. Alone, with nothing in his hands but a flash for light, he was startled by a cry of pain ahead, for he had supposed these forgotten chambers to be empty of all life.

He put out his light, raced ahead on silent feet, guiding himself with a palm against the damp stone wall. A glow of light coming from several openings ahead brought him to a halt. He moved forward more cautiously, peering at last through a grille of ornamental iron, rusted almost away.

The scene before him was startling. There were a dozen of the warrior maids in shining harness, looking like Valkyries with their folded shoulder glide wings. They had opened a concealed trap in the floor and were lowering some bulky mechanical device through it with the aid of ropes.

Gan could not make a move for fear of detection. They were armed and he was alone. He stood motionless and silent, but minutes ticked by and still they struggled with the weight, which seemed too large for the opening. He noted one of the girls had blood on her hand. Obviously the one who had cried out in pain.

He began a slow retreat, trying to steal away as unnoticed

as he had come, only to have his holstered gun strike the wall with a loud thump.

He gave up all caution with the sound and sprinted off, flashing his light ahead for a glimpse of the corridor wall along which he had approached. But, unseen by him, one of the elder Matriarchs had been standing guard at a doorway near the window he had peered through. This officer, leader of the squad of war-maidens, darted out into the center of the corridor, saw his form outlined in his own momentary flash of light.

She fired, and her pellet blasted the pavement from under Gan's flying feet. He took a running dive into a doorway and brought up in the darkness with his head rammed against a soft, cowering form, which whimpered with pain at his impact. He clamped hard hands about a throat and might have hurt her, but instead he relaxed his grip and asked:

"Who are you? Quick!"

"It's only your little Elvir, Captain Gan. I was watching the priestess, and I followed her down here. When I saw what they were doing I started back to get you, but they heard me. I ducked in here and they didn't even look for me. There's a door behind us, but it's locked."

Pushing the girl behind him, Gan fired once into the heavy door. The planks splintered and the thing hung half destroyed. Elvir gave a scream as flying splinters struck around them, but the pillars of the doorway protected them from the blast. Gan put his shoulder to the wreckage and shoved the door open. The hand-flash revealed rows of workbenches, a litter of apparatus long unused, dust and disorder. A dim light hung in the center of the chamber, a worn-out glow lamp such as the Phirans use everywhere, but its light was near useless. Gan realized that this had once been a lavishly fitted laboratory, but was now long abandoned. This was the kind of evidence he was looking for, as

Celys had claimed there was little scientific activity among the Matriarch order.

Racing feet behind them drove them forward into the aisles between the work benches, laden down with glassware, retorts, chemicals in jars, intricate experimental assemblies of tubes and fire-rods and glass containers, electrical wiring and other apparatus whose use and nature were wholly mysterious to Gan's searching eyes.

They crouched out of sight in the aisle between two rows of work benches, listening to the running feet pause at the doorway, then come forward hesitantly into the laboratory where they waited.

Gan peered between the interstices of the apparatus, caught a glimpse of the warrior's harness, that of an officer. Her face was flushed and angry, her pellet gun upraised, her eyes darting about the chamber. Gan could not bring himself to fire, but held his sights on her and waited, thinking how pitiful a culture it was: these lovely creatures trying to repress their own natures and take over all man's duties and ways, with the result that they lived empty lives of envy and hate and a loveless ambition to surpass other women. It just wasn't natural for women to be that way, but then, what man wanted to be a soldier either, at heart?

Step by step she advanced into the room, the shattered door having told her the quarry was here. But her eyes and ears revealed nothing. At last Gan, wearied of the waiting, spoke angrily: "Drop the gun, woman, or I'll have to kill you. I don't want to, you know. I can't get used to the idea of shooting women."

The Amazon whirled, eyes wild with startled fear at the sound of his heavy, dominating voice, and conflict appeared on her face—the desire to drop that gun as she was ordered, the wish not to appear a weak, fearful woman making her clasp the gun more firmly. Her fingers trembled on the heavy saw-grip.

"Drop it, woman. I don't want to hurt you. There's a child with me; you can't fire on me anyway."

At the word *child* the Amazon suddenly relaxed, and Gan realized that he had hit on the one spring that unlocked the Amazons' frozen hearts—they loved children. The gun hand slowly dropped and the gun slipped to the floor.

"Go and pick it up, Elvir, but don't get between us," ordered Gan in a whisper.

Elvir scrambled from under the heavy bench, scuttled across the floor, grabbed up the gun and backed away. Gan stood upright, not ten feet from the Amazon.

"I don't know what you women are trying to do with all this stealing about and trying to kill. You know Phira has fallen, and you know the Tor won't relax his hold on Alid for all your guerilla tactics. Why don't you give up and go back to being women again? Women weren't meant to rule, only to be loved."

HER HEAD reared back, her eyes blazed at him. She was very beautiful in her metal harness, gleamingly polished and jeweled breastplates and the plumes woven into her dark hair. She drew her graceful legs straight under her and assumed a proud carriage as she cried: "We'll never give up while one Matriarch lives."

"It's such a waste," Gan growled. "Could you tell me one good reason for not giving it up?"

"Our knowledge shall not fall into the hands of murderers and thieves...and...*men!* You should be able to understand that the secret is a sacred trust, given to us by the All-Mother."

"Bah!" Gan Alain curled a scornful lip at the officer-maid. "Hypocritical cant. As if you believed that the Matriarch's keeping the secret of longevity from mankind was a good deed!

It's a filthy sample of selfishness in a minority placing its own interests above every other human's health. Now admit it!"

Her head tossed again, for just an instant of angered pride, then the truth of his words and his charge against the Matriarch sank home. Her head lowered in shame. Gan stood, letting her think it out, watching the flush on her cheeks creep higher.

"It shows on your face," Gan said. "Yet you have never admitted it to yourself before."

Her eyes on his became curiously alive with intense inner mental activity. It seemed she was trying to read his mind. At last she sighed, her eyes dropped from his and her head bowed lower. Her voice was muted and soft with deep new emotion.

"Yes, Captain. I have often thought your view might be the correct one, but never allowed myself to admit our wrong. It is so easy to accept teachings one hears all one's life. That is our creed—the dominance of women, the keeping of sciences to the priestesses, the dominance of the Matriarchy over the simpler people of our worlds. But I cannot honestly say that I do not see that our ways are not just or good."

Gan gave a short laugh of triumph. Here was what he had been looking for—one of the leaders who knew the truth, but did not approve of the Matriarchy. Gan moved closer. "Now you're talking sense, and it's the first time I've heard any from these addled females of the temple since I landed on Phira. Now, I'll make you a proposition: reveal this so-sacred secret of life to me, and I'll do my best to get you an adequate reward from the Regent of Konapar."

Her eyes saddened, and the idealistic light fled from her face. Her voice became harsh again, a voice used to command. "I am no traitor, Captain, even though I may not approve of our ways."

"Your oath, I suppose," mused the Cap, aloud. "But have you ever heard of honor? The path of honor for you would seem to dictate that you try to right the ancient wrong these female monopolists have committed, rather than to uphold their crime."

"My name is Aphele, Captain. I have heard of you and know your reputation—all of it." Her eyes twinkled for an instant as she asked: "Are you sure you are completely qualified to talk thus of honor?"

Gan colored, then growled: "I have my code, and I live up to it. Do you? Have you the courage to throw aside your teachings and do the right thing by humanity?"

Her head lifted again in pride. "I have more courage than you, who only pretend to be honest. Suppose I make you a proposition? I will undertake to guide you to a place where the secret you seek may be learned."

"Then there *is* a secret, and it can be learned, can be taught, it's not some miracle of nature..." Gan was thinking aloud, his eyes measuring her, seeing trickery there, wondering how to out-smart her.

"You are afraid," her low, husky voice taunted him. "You fear I would lead you into a trap."

Gan laughed. "You have me in a trap already, Aphele. All you need do is raise your voice and your war-maidens will come running. Is that machine they were working to hide a part of this so-terrific secret?"

Aphele shook her head. "You could kill me before they arrived, and I do not know that you would not. I'll strike a bargain with you: I will not call out, you will go back to the upper levels. An hour from now I will meet you here alone, to take you on a journey of some days duration across the desert land where no man travels. There, in a place forbidden to all men, much can be revealed to you."

IT WAS A MAD proposition; that he should give himself into the keeping of this woman, his life dependent upon her word alone, to be led to what fate he could only imagine. Yet there was a daring challenge on her face, a stirring call to his blood. He knew she was offering him more than her words seemed to indicate. Just what, he could find out only by taking up the challenge. But he did not need to trust her wholly. There were ways unknown to her...

Gan nodded suddenly, his eyes seeming to take fire from her glance: "I'll take your offer, Amazon! I would not wish to place my life's value above that of every human in the galaxy, would you?"

With this parting shot, Gan turned and left, leading little Elvir by the hand. The woman strode after, whispering sharply. "Treachery means death, Captain. You talk of honor, so come in honesty and you will be dealt with honorably."

Gan nodded, did not turn his head. "In one hour I return alone, to see how you keep your word. I may be a fool, but never a coward."

Elvir walked beside him, sobbing little hushed sobs of defeat between clenched teeth. Gan turned and caught her up, holding her face level with his own. "Why the tears, little woman?"

"You've made a date with a sorceress, and you'll never get away from her. You're not mine anymore."

Gan put her down, pausing as he realized the girl knew what was supposed to be a secret to himself alone. Then he laughed and put aside the thought. She would either keep silent or not. It made no difference to him.

CHAPTER NINE

IN HIS quarters, Gan found the Regent of Konapar, seated on Gan's own chair, his fingers drumming impatiently upon the table. "Where have you been keeping yourself, Captain? Rendezvous with some captive Phiran priestess?"

Gan, irked by his attitude, did not smile. "Exactly, your Highness. That is just where I have been. I've arranged a meeting, supposedly with one who will reveal the secret we seek. But I'm under oath not to reveal the matter to you."

The Regent scowled, puzzled. "But you've just broken that oath, haven't you?"

"No. I can't break it until I return. The oath may look different then, you know. They may try to kill me or keep me captive—hard to say what can happen. But I intend to learn whether it is a trap or the genuine thing."

"I'll have you followed. You're a valuable man to me, Captain. I'll not have this."

"Exactly why I brought the matter up at this time. My men will know where I am. There is no need for you to have me followed. You'll have to trust me, Your Highness. It's my neck I'm risking, you know."

The Regent looked thoughtful. "You have a point. If some blunder revealed you were followed by us, it could mean your death, right enough. Very well, Captain. Luck to you. But, to repeat a phrase I picked up from you—don't do it, Captain! Don't even think of it! I'll have you spitted over a slow fire."

Gan laughed. "I'll not keep it from you, Tor Branthak, though I may drive a hard bargain. I'll sell it to you once I get it."

The Tor grimaced. "I'll wager it will cost enough. But then, there's always another means if you prove difficult." His eyes lighted. "After all, we will have two chances. I came here on suspicion, meaning to have it out with you, hammer and tongs. I have just ordered the so-called Supreme Matriarch, that young-looking one, taken to the plateau. There, on my own ship, we can give her a thorough going over with instruments, with truth serum, with lie-detectors, injections of drugs—get the facts out of her."

Gan heaved himself to his feet. Unaccountably, the order for Celys' arrest set his blood afire. Rage choked him. The idea of the noble Matriarch handled like a criminal, given dangerous injections, questioned interminably, put through an inquisition that could well ruin her health or worse, was one he could not accept without emotion. But with an effort he held his tongue until his wits cooled.

The Regent noticed nothing, went on drumming with his fingers on the tabletop. "I've taken quite a fancy to that woman...what's her name now...Celys, Pelys—something. Where the priestesses get their names I can't fathom. They seem to have no family names. The temple is their only family tie. She should make a most ornamental addition to the gems in my harem, if she proves reasonable."

Gan's breath nearly choked him with the hot fire in his lungs. He could not have foreseen this. The man had given no hint of his intentions toward the head Matriarch. Better to wait, bide his time. No good to speak of the thing now.

Gan was having his first full realization of his own attachment to the sharp-tongued Matriarch. This thought struck him, and he relaxed. He nearly smiled as he perceived that there had not been enough between them to give him any confidence that the woman would not prefer the Regent's harem to his own company. She thought of him as an unscrupulous adventurer. Gan stilled his anger, thrust some garments into a small duffel bag, slung it from his shoulder. Clips of pellets for his sidearms completed his preparations. He turned to the Regent and bowed slightly, his smile ironic.

"I trust my departure will cause you no inconvenience, Your Highness. I expect to be gone but a short time, and I hope to find you well on my return. I have your best wishes for success?"

The Regent studied him for a second, then nodded stiffly. "Formality becomes you, Captain. Don't let the plagued women bamboozle you. Get the facts, and let them stuff their ideals and fine talk where it will do most good."

GAN TURNED on his heel and left. But he had no intention of leaving without making sure of something that was bothering him. He moved off toward the Mother's shrine, where he knew Celys might conceal herself in the sanctum if she had heard of the order to arrest her. It could be that she had not been found as yet.

His guess was correct. The Matriarch had been warned by her eavesdropping young acolytes of the order to take her to the plateau outside the city, and had slipped out of her usual regal green ritual robe and donned one of the simpler white gowns belonging to her acolyte, Eloi. Mingling with the chattering groups of adolescents, she was indiscernible to the searching eyes of the soldiery and had escaped recognition for several hours.

But a few hours ago, when they had all filed into the dining hall, one of the guards had recognized her and given a cry of alarm. Celys had fled headlong, dodging through the familiar and intricate passages with the skill of a hunted fox. Darkness had come on, and she had slipped into the great sacred shrine where the dim light and the huge pillars, which supported the dome, gave her effective cover.

The crew of Gan Alain were standing guard at their usual posts, while two-score of the Konaparian warriors scoured the halls and rooms of the temple with search beams in their hands.

Gan paused for a moment beside Chan DuChaile's post before the big arch of the shrine of Myrmi-Atla, and asked a question. "Have they caught the white bird yet, Chan?"

Chan glanced about, shook his head. Then he whispered: "If you're figuring on something else for her, I can tell you where she is, but not for the likes of Tor Branthak."

"I was planning on taking her to the Mother. Do you know what that means?"

Chan nodded, for he had discussed many things with the chattering young girls who were penned in the temple. "She's slipping from pillar to pillar in her own sacred shrine while the Konapar heroes steal about with lights…"

CHAPTER TEN

CELYS crouched behind the great central pillar in the shrine of Myrmi-Atla, watching the swinging lights of the searching Konaparians and praying they would conclude she was not within the darkened shrine and pass on. She shrank back as one small beam swept toward her, then mysteriously blinked out. Feet whispered softly on the stone, and she nearly shrieked as a heavy hand clamped down on her face, shutting off her breath. In her ear a familiar voice whispered.

"Will you be quiet, you beautiful fool? Or must I beat sense through your hide with a whip? I am your friend. Now, tell me, how do we get out of this place before some of the Regent's men spot you?"

The hand slowly released its powerful grasp and Celys shuddered as breath came back into her lungs. The beast was still trying to trick her with his honest blue eyes, with his heart-ensnaring curls and fearful brawny arms about her. There was nothing he would not stoop to! What was she to do? She who had thought men so simple and easy to fool before—and this one was not fooled in the least, whatever his game. If only he was what he seemed, an honest, strong man trying to do the right thing, rather than an amorous beast trying to undo her reason with his love-making in order to secure the ancient secret from her.

Celys, in a sudden flash of hatred for all things masculine and alien, tugged out a little dagger from a hidden sheath.

Her hand drew back, darted forward, and Gan's hand caught her wrist just as the point touched his throat. A few drops of blood stained her wrist as she twisted, and the knife dropped with a sinister tinkling on the floor between them.

Gan had half a mind to call out and bring the searchers down upon her, but he growled softly into her ear: "For a woman who is unable to resist my arms, you show small gratitude for my affection. I come to help you escape the Regent's third-degree, and you try to knife me. Are you just a common murderess, and not the high-minded woman I thought?"

Celys was sincerely thankful the blade had done no harm. The spasm of rage had passed, and she realized she was near the breaking point from strain, or she would never have done such a thing. Tears came to her eyes, and at the same time anger burned in her cheeks, trembled in her hands—anger at her own impotence against these males from another world. She wanted so very much to believe in this man beside her, yet she felt certain he was but a scoundrel who mimicked the ways of honor to betray her.

Gan murmured: "Lead the way to the secret passages that lead from this temple. I have a way of contacting your forces—in fact, a guide is even now awaiting me in the subterranean passages."

Celys nodded her head in mute acquiescence, her eyes on his with something of final defeat in them. Gan knew that it was the defeat of an overweening feminine pride, which could not bear to think of any man as superior. Her voice was very weak, whispering into his ear.

"Forgive me. I'm half out of my mind with strain. You embodied all the indignities I have suffered—I am not myself. I would have escaped long since through a passage nearby, but I have not been able to approach the entrance, as there has always been somebody about. Come…"

GAN TOOK her hand and let her guide him through the dimness. Then he saw her reason for choosing the shrine of the All-Mother's image for her hiding place. She pressed a carved ornament in the stone of a pillar pedestal and a segment of the pillar opened out. They slipped inside and Celys pulled the false stone back into place. The pillar itself was the top of a tiny stairway, so narrow that Gan had trouble squeezing his great shoulders past the winding steps that circled a center pole. Celys giggled audibly at his contortions.

"This wasn't meant for a fat Matriarch..."

"May you never grow fat...you are perfect as you are," he said, grunting.

Her eyes danced, but he did not know if it was because of his contorted face as he wriggled his way downward, or because of the compliment.

At the bottom Gan paused to readjust his leather corselet. There he discovered the woman had found opportunity to lift one of his pellet guns from his belt. Gan shivered with sudden apprehension for if she meant to kill him, one of his own guns would prove more efficient than the slender blade with which she had failed.

"Better give me the gun, sister. It was never meant for female hands."

Her laugh was mocking, cool and quite possessed. "So now it's 'sister'? I have become younger since last night? Do you no longer consider me motherly?"

"The gun!" growled Gan, frowning. "You're much too impulsive with weapons to carry them about so carelessly."

"*You* have a weapon. *I* have a weapon. What could be fairer?"

Gan shrugged, his eyes meeting only a rather charming expression of deviltry in hers. Then he said: "Well, keep it.

But let me warn you, the triggers have been filed. They're about half the standard pull. Also, there's another thing I must speak to you about. I had a similar altercation with one of your associates. She is waiting now in the subterranean passages to guide me to the Mother. She has my word of honor to reveal nothing of what I learn without permission, and I have hers for my safety. Now that you've led me into this secret passage of yours, you will have to guide me to her."

Rather abruptly she shoved the gun, which she had been holding behind her, toward him. "In that case, take your ugly weapon. I will have no need of it. The mother will decide your fate when we reach Avalaon. Come…"

Gan lifted the weapon gingerly from her hand, for it was actually hair-triggered, and she hadn't handled it too gently. In her hands, it would have been more dangerous to her than to him.

The beautiful Matriarch laughed again at his tense expression, then turned and moved off into the darkness. Here and there along the narrow passages little glow lamps were set, and Gan tried to figure his distance and position in the temple by the distance between lights. But he was hopelessly lost in the twisting of the narrow passage within the walls.

In short minutes she slid open a panel, let him out into the underground chambers where he had left the Amazon, Aphele. She was waiting there, concealed by the shadows, alone. She moved out into the dim light.

"I thought you'd never come…"

Gan grunted. "I had to rescue the soubrette of the cast. The Tor was about to give her a going over. I suppose you know the Supreme Matriarch?"

Aphele darted to the open panel, where Celys stood, and the two women touched hands for an instant. Aphele turned back to Gan Alain. "Must she flee? Her Supremity is needed here. I don't understand."

Celys moved forward, facing Aphele. "Where have you undertaken to lead this man, Lieutenant? Not to Avalaon?"

Aphele stood proudly, facing her superior. "I realize the risk. But I believe he might be convinced when he knows all. It is worth trying."

Celys shook her head. "He is but the captain of a single ship, an adventurer of no influence, a mere mercenary under Tor Branthak's command. What good could he do our cause?"

The two women stood facing each other, and what passed between them was mysterious to Gan, for Celys turned away, shrugged, said: "Very well, I have nothing to say. But you are playing with a fire that is apt to burn more than you think."

Almost immediately Lieutenant Aphele drew her pellet gun, leveled it at Gan. "Your weapons, Captain. I am sorry if I led you to believe you would not be my captive."

Gan gave them up.

NOW THE two women rather pointedly ignored him, and after they caught up with the waiting troops and Gan found himself marching in the center of a score of well-armed and well-disciplined warrior women, he rather doubted his own good sense.

Gan realized that the Matriarch's disappearance, coinciding with his own departure, was going to place Tor Branthak's trust of him under a strain. But the chances were he'd never have to worry about that. What really worried him were his men and his ship. It would have been best if he had demanded his share of the wealth of Alid and left immediately after the city had fallen. But he had been drawn by the damned *secret* and he doubted more strongly every moment that there *was* any secret.

The march continued for what Gan judged was an hour, perhaps some four miles of underground tunnels. Then they entered a line of monorail cars suspended from the ceiling of the tunnel. Gan reasoned that they left the cars outside the city because of the possible sound their use might make under the foundations.

The train was light and fast, designed for passenger use only. Gan judged they traveled around sixty miles an hour for several hours. Then the tunnel ended, but before ascending a ramp into the open air, the women donned garments of rough skins and sand hoods of soft leather. These were the garments of the wild nomads of the deserts of Phira, and at the surface a herd of the horse-like beasts called *morts* was awaiting them.

From the air, the party would resemble any other mounted party of nomads and would cause no unwanted inquiry from the Konaparian scout planes patrolling the planet for possible organized resistance.

"Is the place distant?" asked Gan of Aphele, who rode beside him. Celys had taken her place at the head of the column, riding beside the officer who headed the detachment. Aphele twitched the head of her pop-eyed, horned mount closer to him and smiled as she lifted back the hood from her ears to reveal her wealth of soft brown hair.

"Two days ride, Captain. Unless you are accustomed to riding, you will have calluses where none were before."

Gan shook his head. "I have never ridden anything not on wheels or jets before. I think I know what you mean already."

The woman's eyes were humorously sympathetic. "You will not enjoy the next two days, Captain. You will need whatever stoicism your nature provides."

Gan, already appreciating the monotony of the repeating

dunes and the irritating qualities of sand down his neck, decided that the best way to ignore the unpleasantness was to keep on talking. He was somewhat nettled by the obvious dislike of himself expressed by the warrior women's concerted disregard of his presence. He threw back his own hood, letting the sun shine on his golden curls.

"Have you made this trip often, Aphele?"

"Hundreds of times, Captain. In the last hundred years, I have passed this way at least once every two years."

GAN GULPED. So this was another of the long-lived breed, according to Celys' version of the secret. She looked about twenty-two. The Phiran year was but ten days shorter than the Terran year, and the day was some two hours longer. Gan glanced up at the bright orange double star that served both Konapar and Phira as a sun. Menkis, they called it. On the charts it was labeled Menanger.

"What was that device you and your friends were lowering through the floor when you shot at me?" he asked, watching her face closely. She did not even look at him, watching instead the flight of a gold and blue bird hovering above their heads. Her voice was a discreet murmur, audible not three feet away.

"It was part of the secret which we did not wish the Konaparians to discover, as you suspect."

Gan felt a swift elation surge through him. So she was a convert to his way of thinking; was a friend and ally against the secretive selfishness of these so-holy priestesses.

Then she turned her head and laughed, and spoke more loudly. "What did you say? I am so sleepy…"

He spoke loudly himself. "Aren't you sorry you shot at me last night? You might have killed me."

Her eyes danced. "Oh, I could have, but you are too good-looking to kill. I meant only to take some of the smugness out of you."

"You did," Gan laughed. "I will admit that women can do as good a job of soldiering as men, and but short weeks ago I thought differently."

Aphele twitched the mort's ugly head closer again. She whispered: "I am sick to death of hearing the two sexes compared. Never mention it to me again. Do you hear?"

"No sex conversation? What will we talk about?"

Aphele frowned. "That is not what I meant, and you know it. On Phira, when a woman decides she wants a Phiran male, she tells him so. I understand that, with Terrans, the opposite is true and the woman must never mention the subject closest to her heart, but wait for the man to speak his love."

Gan nodded, his eyes on hers doubtfully. He read the signs aright—she was his friend, and more! Up to now it had been his custom to avoid too close entanglement with any female. They had always meant trouble. Now it seemed he was in trouble again... But there was an honesty and candor on her face—and Aphele was not only very lovely, but she was also a woman who had already lived several lifetimes. Perhaps her mind, also, was so far ahead of his in perception that she knew exactly what he thought. Certainly the simple directness in her meant profound knowledge of the human mind rather than simplicity.

He asked: "You have lived so much longer than I, you should have greater wisdom, should be able to guess my every thought before I speak; can you tell me what I'm thinking?"

Though she looked at him whimsically, her lips gave a bitter twist. "I know you're afraid to have me say I am attracted to you. I know you are not affected by my beauty. I know that the first Matriarch is in your heart. But listen to me, Terran. Sometimes it is better to be loved than to love.

I, at least, would be your friend, and I would expect no lease on your life in return. You know nothing of the nature of my mind. I can be more to you than she—if you will allow yourself to understand."

GAN WAS struck by her serious tone, as well as by the thread of her speech. But another thing occupied his attention: "You say the first Matriarch. Who is that? I had thought Celys was the Supreme Matriarch."

"There are several who play the part of the Supreme Matriarch. She is but a figurehead. The real power rests in the ancient one we travel to consult. She holds the keys to the mystery, the secret you seek. I want to guide you correctly, so that it may be possible for you to live beside me. You see, Terran, I have lost two mates in the years long past, because the secret is denied to males."

Her countenance was a bitter mask of strange loneliness for a second, and Gan realized that living for centuries was perhaps not all peaches and cream. Then the expression passed, and she smiled again, perhaps at his suddenly lugubrious expression over hearing of her former mates.

"You needn't fear me, Gan. I am an experienced woman, who has long ago given up the childish tricks by which young women gain their ends. If you need me, come to me. I will not pursue you."

She twitched at her mount's reins, as if to ride ahead beyond earshot. Gan reached out and seized the mort's reins in one big hand.

"You have read my mind, Aphele, and answered my questions. Can you also read the admiration and liking I have for you?"

She settled back, her face relaxed from its bitterness as he went on: "I want to know one more thing, and then no more questions. Has Celys been married too, lost her mates the same way? Is she, too, centuries old?"

She laughed at his intent face; a laugh at once mocking and tender, as with a child. "You have a disappointment in store, my friend. Your Celys is not one, but several. Their ages are not young or old, for they are daughters each of the other. All of them are older than you, and have children. There is one, the youngest of the Matriarch line, who is but twice your age. You haven't met her, yet you would know her surely, so closely does she resemble her grandmother."

Gan turned toward the erect figure of Celys ahead. "Her grandmother! A grandmother, that one ahead?" He said it with a kind of dismayed awe.

Aphele nodded, her eyes pitying, her lips twisted in a kind of sad smile. "That is why I tried to tell you, a love such as I offer you is at least less confusing than that which you are bent on pursuing. There is but one of me, and I am not too proud to say you are a man above men, and above most women I have known. Now I leave you to your thoughts."

She rode ahead, to pause beside the stiff, slender figure of Celys. Gan burned with curiosity to hear what they were saying, and if it concerned him. He knew that if he saw them laugh, he would feel like a fool. Just then the two women laughed and glanced back at him and he felt like a fool.

CHAPTER ELEVEN

AT LAST the long and arduous trip in the saddle came to an end and they came to the hidden valley of Avalaon. It was a place of trees, tremendous in size. Cedars or redwoods, or some relative of the conifers, towered in aged splendor toward the sky, rich in foliage and mighty in trunk. That there was a city beneath the trees would have been indistinguishable from the air, and Gan could see that great care had been taken to have no trails or roads leading into the valley. The mouth of the valley was a hilly pass, also heavily wooded, and it could have been defended by one man with an automatic rifle, as the sides were precipitous.

Winding down the faintly worn pathways into the dim depths of the wooded valley, Gan did not expect to find any great number of people or any structures, but he was surprised to find the flourishing city whose extent was difficult to estimate, so the forest growth obscured the vistas. The dwellings were built beneath the trees; several small streams wound about through them and joined in a river that seemed to end in a lake in the center of the valley. The houses were of stone, permanent and old-looking, as if they had been there undisturbed for centuries. But they were lived in, for figures moved along the paths beneath the trees carrying burdens of food or clothing or small cases of metal articles.

Aphele dismounted as they reached the first of these hidden dwellings, and came back to Gan, holding the mort's head as he dismounted.

"How is your backside?" she asked, smiling.

"I am more conscious of its presence than ever before," grinned Gan, bending and stretching.

"You are now in a place never before reached by the uninitiated," she said, her eyes measuring him with evident delight in her glance, a look full of desire and appreciation of his masculinity. "I am responsible for your being here, so if you have a care for my welfare, conduct yourself accordingly. No male has trod these paths for many centuries—since before we can remember. The sacred groves of Myrmi-Atla have been entered only by women who have passed very stringent examinations and undergone long purification. You may be slain, you know, before I have a chance to make a case for you. I have long been a dissident from the idea of complete female supremacy, and am known as a rebel. Though there are others, we are in the minority. We want men in the organization, we need men. The others will not have it. There is much politics involved, but I will advise you. I am taking you to our true head, who has no title. She is over five hundred years old."

Gan nodded, feeling like a folly-stricken idiot treading where only angels would dare.

The warrior women shed the ugly and bad-smelling disguises, throwing them in a heap where Gan had doffed his own cloak and hood.

SEVERAL slight figures appeared from among the nearby trees and approached. Gan started as he realized they were young girls and quite naked. They came forward in innocent shamelessness, but suddenly one of them saw Gan's stalwart male figure with the curling red-gold beard proclaiming his essential masculinity. The girl gave a scream of utter horror, as if she were confronted by a banshee, and took to her heels. In an instant the grove was filled with the small naked figures running and screaming as the others saw the cause of the initial fright. The scream brought still more naked young nymphs, who came running up. When they saw the great man-figure with the beard, they ran away as quickly as they had come.

There was not a laugh or an expression in the whole troop of warrior women at this development. It was evident that they had expected it. There were several frowning glances at Aphele, who ignored them. Gan saw that her idea of bringing him here was disapproved by many.

"No good can come from this violation of the inviolate grove of Avalaon," one of them said coldly to Aphele as they passed her with the saddles of their beasts. They had turned the beasts loose in the forest.

Gan, weaponless, was appreciating to the full the chances of his death now mentioned for the first time by Aphele. But he strode along beside her, just behind the tall and graceful form of Celys, who was still the center of attraction to him in spite of her newest character of grandmother to a woman who resembled her so closely as to be identical.

They passed several of the small stone houses and came to a much larger structure, placed between four of the forest giants so closely that the mighty trunks seemed to uphold the walls and roof. The guarding troop stopped and lined up on each side of the low, wide doorway of plain, rough timbers, deeply marked by time. Gan passed between them with somewhat the feeling of a criminal entering a jail, and the glittering uniforms and stern, if beautiful, faces of the women made him feel guilty for being a man.

Inside the rather dimly lit room there were several women working at desks and file cases, and a score of others seated on benches about the walls. The women at the desks were the first elderly women wearing the regalia of the priestesses of Myrmi-Atla that Gan had seen. These, in a Terran civilization, would have been women of sixty or sixty-five. Here, Gan had no idea of their ages.

In the center of the low-ceilinged place was a rough wooden dais and high-backed chair on, which sat a woman Gan would have recognized as the leader without a nudge from Aphele. The high dome of white brow, the weary-wise eyes, the strong mouth and chin, the proud look of her—Gan moved forward with Aphele and knelt on one knee, as did his mentor.

The woman, showing her great age in a mass of wrinkles, but otherwise appearing to be very strong and able, inclined her head, studying them with her face bearing a slight smile. Her voice was high-pitched, but full; a firm and even musical voice.

"Aphele, you have led one of the enemy here?" Her voice was gently chiding. "Can you justify the indiscretion?"

APHELE stood, thrust her high bosom out, and lifted one hand in a gesture of complete confidence.

"The conqueror, Tor Branthak of Konapar, seeks the secret. He hired this pirate captain to obtain it for him without his followers' knowing. Since of course he could unearth no secret, Tor Branthak has ordered the torture of the Supreme Matriarch until she tells. This man rescued our first Celys from her peril, brought her to me, came with us of his own free will. The rest is up to you and our council. I will have more to say in council and you already know my opinions on the matter of secrecy."

The old leader smiled and nodded. "We all know your opinions, Aphele, and none will accuse you of secrecy about them. You shout them out at every opportunity. So, he is not a captive nor yet a hostage, but merely a curious gentleman who wants to see for himself how we stay alive?"

Aphele did not answer, but stepped back one pace with smart military bearing, standing very erect and still. This left Gan facing the old leader of the Amazons alone, and a little sweat broke out on his brow as the thought came to him that he was facing a person whose mind had been pitted against all men for some five centuries—and had won. Gan kept his eyes on hers unwaveringly, his face quite empty of expression, but he could not control the nerves of his hands, which kept opening and closing as if to grasp some material thing to aid him in this predicament.

The voice of the old woman took on a deeper note, a rasping, critical, angry tone of disapproval.

"Do you realize that these groves of Avalaon have not been violated by man's presence for near a thousand years? And now you come blundering in where the last strength of the female lords of Phira licks its wounds, expecting mercy and benevolence and perhaps romance from our so-pretty warrior maids? You are a bigger fool than the woman who brought you!"

An angry exhalation from the two-score female breasts in the room emphasized her words. It was a long, deep sigh, a kind of "aye", and it meant unanimous agreement with her. Gan, startled, let his glance sweep the room, where more and more of the women were clustering, as the curious took note of the strange meeting. Peeping between the red-uniformed legs of the guard at the door were a score of naked young nymphs, their mouths round with astonishment and fascination. Gan felt more out of place and off balance than he had ever been in his life. He opened his mouth to speak and found himself only able to croak, "Er...ah..." in a dismal sound like a sick frog.

The old woman relaxed suddenly, her hands dropping from their grip on the chair's rough wood arms, and leaned back. Then her voice became humorous. Sarcastically she mimicked him: "The man says, 'er...ah...' If that is not profound wisdom, indeed! Can you summon no defense, can you think of no good reason why our privacy and isolation should be destroyed by you? Off with you, then, while we take thought of your fate."

Then Gan found his voice, and all of it came boiling up; the many little insults and derogation's these women had handed him since he set foot on Phira became a torrent of resentment, and he let out a great bellow such as had made his crew run rather than face him.

"Now listen to me. I've been insulted and chivvied about and made to feel foolish ever since I first met the so-holy priestesses of your All-Mother. I took it like a man, and was courteous and kind and tried my best to protect them from the soldiers of Konapar, and wasn't even thanked by one of you until I met Aphele. I saved your precious Celys from torture the first day on this planet, and had it put off from day to day until I contrived her escape. I have been the good friend of you high-nosed females at the risk of my own precious neck, and now you laugh at me. I am beginning to think the men who say that woman's place is in the hearth, kitchen and bedroom are right. It's a new idea to me, because I've always observed women's low estate on many barbarous planets with great pity. However, perhaps it is the nature of a woman to abuse power even more than men. It seems you enjoy the idea of having the whiphand over a male."

HIS ROARING voice, bringing with it the vast sense of space and the adventurous, roving life he had led, huge and strong and filled with masculine power and anger, filled with righteousness and indignation and contempt of the petty intentions of these women to shoot their barbed arrows of scorn into him, expressing the rage at his treatment, did far more for him than any argument in words. When his voice ceased, there was a silence as if a god had spoken, and from each female breast there came a sigh, of longing at last realized, a desire at last gratified—to hear a male voice raised in the forest aisles of Avalaon.

The old leader's eyes glittered like diamonds in her face as she looked about at the bemused countenances of the men-starved women about her, each rapt as if still hearing the great male sound of Gan Alain roaring his rage. Whether they were glittered with tears or with an evil anger, Gan could not tell. She said nothing in reply, but only waved a hand to Aphele, who tugged at Gan's sleeve of worn gold leather and led him out into the bright, clean air where the piney scent of the forest breathed silence and peace.

"You," murmured Aphele, her eyes glowing, "are a man after my heart. You really gave it to her and the rest of them. They are too long in the saddle to understand that the worlds were not exactly made just for the purpose of organizing women into trampling upon all men. Ah, it was worth the long ride to hear it!"

They had been walking now alone through the trees, and Aphele stopped him. "Now give me a good hard hug and a kiss, as if I were some sweet damsel you knew when you were young enough to think of nothing but kissing girls..."

Gan was not taken unawares by her request, but still he hesitated. Then he remembered how it used to be, when he was a boy walking in the evening with his chosen, how sweet a kiss could be—and he seized her and held her close, bent back her fair face and kissed her heartily. It was sweet, bittersweet, full of memories of other loves, and none of them quite measuring up to Aphele's deep, hungry eyes, nor her strange mouth, so sweet and hungry, yet so sorrowful.

Her smile after the kiss was not the twisted smile she usually gave him, but a full and grateful thanks. Her voice was husky and low as she said: "Oh, it is good, even as it used to be when I believed in love and life and men. You are a man such as I have always longed for but never did quite believe existed. I put a spell upon you, Gan Alain—may you never forget the lips of Aphele, no matter the years or the space between us."

A low and scornful voice behind them made them both whirl, and standing there was Celys, saying: "Not long ago you were making love to me—Celys! Now you are embracing Aphele. What is a woman to think?"

Gan was angry. He gave a short, hard laugh. "Not long ago I did not know you were grandmother to a grown woman, Celys. May I meet the other Supreme Matriarchs?"

Celys flushed angrily, and her hand pointed suddenly at Aphele, her fist clenching tight. "You told him, you ancient thing, to get him for yourself! You know there's not a male like him on all Phira, and I have had his declaration first. I'll get even with you, Aphele! Wait."

Gan stood, somewhat dismayed at her display, and feeling that this was none of his argument. But Aphele needed no help.

"You made him unhappy with your disregard. Now you claim him, after he gives his kiss to me. There was no reason to think you ever wanted the man. I have not claimed him, I only kissed him. Terrans believe in freedom, not chains; and if I know him, he will prefer my freedom to your dominance, my dear superior."

"That could well be, Celys," growled Gan, seeing now what Aphele had been telling him all along—these women thought they must dominate all things.

Aphele sensed his thought. "They would brand men like horses, Gan, and sometimes do." She went on, coloring as her circulation caught up with her anger. "They think marriage is a thing for a man to wear like a dog collar around his neck, instead of a glorious partnership and a joyous one."

CHAPTER TWELVE

GAN'S FIRST day in Avalaon drew to a close, and Aphele led him to an empty cabin beneath the trees, lit a fire in the rude stone fireplace, left him to his own devices. Almost exhausted, Gan drew off his boots, pulled a fur over himself and went to sleep on the rustic bunk built into the wall.

Some hours later he was awakened by the sound of giggling and soft footsteps. He sat up to find himself surrounded by the naked young girls who had at first shown such horror at his presence. They stood in a circle about his bunk, ranging from tiny tots to girls in their teens, peering at him in the dim firelight and discussing his appearance in excited whispers. One of them, older and bolder than the rest, stepped up.

"You are the first man we ever saw, and we want to

apologize for our discourtesy this afternoon."

Gan grunted, slightly irritated to be the cynosure of so many eyes, and awakened thus for mere curiosity, and slightly embarrassed as his eyes roved over the slim but womanly body of the one who had addressed him. Then he realized that hers was source of information not so likely to be close-mouthed as the older women.

"You children are apt to get yourself into trouble if you're caught here, to say nothing of me. But now that you're here, I'll give you a few minutes. Ask me any questions you want, and I'll answer, provided you answer some of mine in return."

The lovely heads nodded soberly, like angels gathered about a bier; and Gan wondered if that weren't pretty close to the truth. One asked: "You're from the Terran worlds, where men and women are equal. It must be fun to live that way, with boys and girls together."

"It is fun," answered Gan. "They don't run about exactly as you do, but they play together, and they are very happy. Tell me, don't you ever see boys at all?"

"Never, not until mating time. That's every two years, in the Fall, when the grown women chose a mate for three months. We see some of the boys then, but we daren't play with them or talk with them." There was a wistful note in the girl's voice as she stood there unabashed. "It seems wrong..."

"It is wrong," said Gan. "The whole idea is wrong, to my way of thinking. Men and women are happier when they live together."

"The old women are strict and mean and never let us have any real fun. What's the fun of being young if you never see a boy?"

Gan's heart went out to her suddenly. Here was one girl who really needed her first kiss. All at once he felt that if it was the last thing he did on this planet, or any other, he would smash this Matriarchy and set this one, and the others like her, free to enjoy the fruits she so desperately needed.

"Where do they keep all the men on Phira, anyway? I have seen very few since I've been here."

"They keep them in a place like this on the other side of the planet, except the ones who work as servants in the homes of the officials and tradespeople. It is a place called Manoa. There all young boys are taken and must stay until they grow up."

Gan growled. "A completely unnatural arrangement, contrary to nature. No wonder your elders grow to be psychotic. So there are only servants in the dwellings in the cities? No man-and-wife teams running the homes?"

"Oh, some break the rules and keep their men at home; but they have to keep pretty well under cover and not be seen often. According to the law, mating season lasts but three months, and then the man must go back to Manoa."

"Servants and studs," growled Gan angrily, looking over the serious young faces gathered close about his bed. "A sad thing you have made of men on Phira, eh?"

"It is not us," they chorused. "We think it is a sad thing, too. But the old laws and customs are so rigid, how could they be changed?"

GAN'S EYES widened. There were more "rebels" in the Matriarch camp than perhaps even the Matriarchy realized. "On Terran worlds," said Gan, "in the olden times, they would have elected a new government, new officials, passed new laws to suit themselves. Nowadays, since the Empire has been established, this is not so easy. But it is still done. Do you know what an election is?"

"No, we don't."

"Well." Gan looked at them sharply, "it's very simple. It

means that you select a number of persons whom you'd like to govern you, then you vote among yourselves. The winner, the one with the most votes, becomes your ruler and she then rules you according to your group desires. That way you have laws that you like, and obey willingly."

A low whistle from outside sent the girls scurrying through the door, and in an instant the cabin was as empty as before. None too soon, for the sound of boots came up a pathway, and the door was flung open. A light flashed inside, an older woman's voice asked: "Is everything all right, Terran? I thought I saw movement about the cabin."

"Everything's all right," growled Gan, sleepily. "You woke me up, is all..."

The woman shut the door and went on along her rounds. For a few minutes Gan lay idly wondering, and was dropping off to sleep again when the door was opened stealthily and a slight figure came in clumsily, bearing several chunks of wood. These she put on the fire, then came to his bedside. Her whisper was husky. "We thought you might be chilly, you being from another world."

Gan looked at her, slender and beautiful as hand-rubbed marble, her dark eyes two question marks of youthful innocence in the firelight. She stood there unabashed, and after a few seconds crept closer until her body touched Gan's hand where it lay along the side of the bunk.

"Tell me more," she whispered. "Tell me about men. We talk and talk among ourselves, but we really know so little, and it's all so confusing."

Gan bunched up his surcoat, which he had balled under his head for a pillow, so that his eyes were near level with hers.

"More talk from me would do you little good, girl. Your problem is one that plagues all youth, and nothing but time and experience will cure your ailment."

"Then show me," she begged, her lips pouting prettily. "Just show me what a kiss is like, and what love might be when I grow old enough to mate."

GAN GASPED, but the sweet young eyes begging of him what he was not unwilling to give were too much. He reached out and tugged her angelic young face close and touched his lips to hers, or meant to. But she pressed forward, clasped him tight, and her lips were burning hot on his, her young body shivering with delight under his hands. Abruptly he pushed her back and she stood with hands clasped together, her breath panting in rapture, her eyes dewed with wonder.

"So that is a kiss! It's wonderful. Love must be wonderful..."

Gan decided to stick strictly to words from here on, and pulled up his furs close about him.

"Yes, love can be wonderful, girl, when it comes to you. And if the rule of the Matriarchy can be broken, you'll have a chance to find it, which you have precious little as things stand. It is the lack of a solution to your problem, which has embittered the old women about you. If I have my way..."

"I can help you," she whispered, her eyes glowing. "They mean to kill you, soon. First they will have a meeting, and pretend it is all legal and right. But they will decide you must die, as all men must die who find their way here, so that the sanctuary will stay hidden from men."

Gan scowled and whispered: "I had guessed as much when I first set eyes upon the old shrew whom you call Mother. But what puzzles me, is what can I do about it now? There is no way of escape open to me."

"There is a way. If you accept one of the warrior maids in marriage. The law is so worded that they cannot kill a mate. They can beat you, but not kill."

Gan smiled grimly. "I doubt if they will allow me time or opportunity for that."

"I could hide you," the girl went on in an earnest whisper. "I know this forest well, and there are places where they would not find you easily. It would take many days, and we could keep on fleeing, on and on…"

"What would happen to you, sweet one, if we were caught?"

She hung her head. "If they did not sentence me to death, they would banish me to the desert, which is almost as certain."

Gan shook his head. "I'm afraid I will have to use my own devices, little angel. Go now, and don't worry about me. My own gods will care for me where your All-Mother will not. I will be safe. Go."

The girl went hesitantly, pausing to peer back at him in the flickering firelight, lovely in her pity and concern and her innocent nudity, so that Gan's heart went out to her as his own daughter. Then she closed the door and was gone.

Gan flicked the switch on the radio device upon his belt. He knew that, on his ship, Chan DuChaile would be waiting, tubes set for super-sensitivity, and would not miss a whisper.

"Listen, Chan; try to get the ship aloft unobserved, and then home on this wave until it's beneath you. Then wait. When I shut off the wave, come down with your guns peeled for trouble."

Gan repeated the message a half-dozen times, at intervals of fifteen minutes. Then he drifted off to sleep much easier in his mind.

IN THE morning Gan Alain was awakened by the voice of Aphele, calling from outside. Gan slipped on his boots, opened the door to her. She had removed the masculine uniform with its harsh steel breast and abdomen plates, and was wearing instead a kind of sarong which left her breasts bare, and on her soft, floating hair a wreath of wood flowers gave her a dryad look of extreme attractiveness. Gan flushed guiltily at sight of her, for some reason he himself could not understand.

"It is good," said Aphele in a husky voice, "to dress as a woman and to wake a man with one's heart knocking at one's ribs. I had almost forgotten how good it could be. I give you good morning, and hope you will live the day out."

He grimaced, and she laughed, but not without worry.

"The council seems set upon your death, even though I am correct in guaranteeing your life and liberty under the normal status of a military truce. They are a bunch of abnormal old biddies, who see only evil in all men and most things related to sex."

"I may have a surprise for them," said Gan. "If they violate my neutrality; if they threaten me or take steps to execute me, I think they will find that I am not so helpless as they think."

Aphele pressed close against him, taking his hand. "Walk with me, and murmur sweet words into my ears. Gan, the forest is lovely at this time of year."

Gan moved out into the daylight, and the smell of cooking meat gave him hunger pangs. He groaned. "Aphele, never expect a man to make love on an empty stomach. And in the morning, of all times, a man cannot even be courteous until he has been fed. Do you know nothing of the male whatever?"

She laughed and pointed. "I have built a fire, and what you smell is your meat cooking. The others will eat in their barracks, where you are not allowed. Come, or you get no breakfast."

Gan put his arm about her waist and moved toward the fire between the vast boles of the ancient trees. Her laughter and her beauty made the forest seem twice as lovely as yesterday. The breakfast she had prepared was very fine.

"You do understand the animal, man, after all, don't you?" Gan said, his mouth full of deer meat.

THE COUNCIL, called in midmorning, was out in the open air. There were several thousand females, of various ages, gathered on the grass and leaf mold of the forest aisles, watching the ceremonial chair placed for the Mother. Watching the twenty other women seated at a long table of planks, before which Gan stood, like a criminal before the bar, there was little doubt as to their undivided opinion.

There was little ceremony wasted on the proceedings. Aphele was called to testify, and she told the simple truth: that she had thought the council might wish to barter the ancient secret Tor Branthak sought for the freedom of Phira, and therefore she had brought this man to negotiate the deal.

Celys was called, and for the first time Gan saw the three identical women, daughter, mother and grandmother, who had played Supreme Matriarch for the hidden council for some four centuries, according to Aphele's whispered information. To Gan's eyes, they were equally beautiful, the grandmother somewhat more mature in proportions, but all three would have been taken for young women on any other world.

Celys testified to her part in the journey, and that Gan had been instrumental in her escape, if not essential. No one spoke a word against him, at first. After the two women had spoken, Gan found himself facing the old leader across the plank table.

"It has been our custom for ages," she began, her eyes glittering out of her wrinkled face and her lips straight and thin and hard, clipping off her words with machine precision, "to slay all men who found their way to this sanctuary of womanhood. In the ancient times men were put to the death under the great fission ray. This ray was emitted from a great mechanical device known only to the Matriarchs of Myrmi-Atla. I, myself, was known to have pushed men into this ray of death—a ray that incinerated the very flesh it touched. Their seared bodies were blasted into a great vat, within which their remains were dissolved. But now, after centuries, it is proposed that the ancient customs by which we live, customs which are time-hallowed laws, be set aside; that they be set aside because of the present crisis, the downfall of Alid, the defeat of our space fleet, the inrush of alien troops into our cities. It is proposed, moreover, that they be set aside in a cowardly act of barter, a barter in which we give immortality, our greatest single treasure, to the enemy in return for a dubious promise of immunity from their avowed plan of complete destruction of the power of Myrmi-Atla. I am ardently against this proposal. But the council may decide, and I will abide by their wishes, as always."

Gan was not asked to say a word in his defense. The old woman gave the nod to the women gathered about the table, who at once began to pass little slips of folded paper the length of the table, where they were gathered by the woman at the head of the table. She copied off the total of votes upon the papers and, after a moment, arose, facing Gan, who stood at the farther end of the table. Her voice was as impersonal and empty of human concern for Gan as a voice record.

"The council has voted, and the decision is death."

Gan swung about, and his hand went to his belt, shutting off the self-contained power unit, which energized the little wave-generator in his belt. In an instant two tall, uniformed warrior maids sprang to his side, seized his arms, thinking to hold him.

Gan was furious at the prearranged inevitability of the

"trial" and the way in which it was run off without discussion or proper consideration of all the factors involved.

He twisted one arm loose from the maid on his right, seized the other about the waist, holding her between himself and the other. In two swift movements he had seized her pellet gun and ring thrower, and as the other maid reached over to strike him with the long dagger, which was the only weapon she could use safely here in the midst of thousands of innocent bystanders, he inadvertently held the woman in his arms between himself and the dagger so that she thrust it into her comrade's breast.

The warrior maid sprang back at this sudden development, the bloody dagger in her hand, and her distraught face making the whole scene plain to the observers as in a drama.

Gan dropped the wounded woman, fitted a ring into the ring-thrower and faced the council table with the weapon, ready to toss the deadly fission ring directly into the midst of the council.

"We will now proceed to hold trial correctly," bellowed Gan. "Or else you can all immediately go up in the air in tiny pieces and we can elect a new council more to a man's liking. All of you not in favor may signify by remaining standing. The others, please be seated, as you see your wise old leader already doing."

It took them all of ten seconds to get the order through their heads and resume their seats. Cap motioned with his weapon to Aphele.

"My dear lady, since you seem the only one here with human blood in your veins, will you preside in place of the old lady who prefers murder to legal procedure?"

Aphele's hand went to her mouth in sincere fear of the consequences of such an act, but Gan was adamant.

"You will note, Aphele, that the old woman has already made her seat vacant for you. Please take your place."

Aphele, knowing he had them all at his mercy with the explosive ring, capable of blowing the whole council table and all its members up in one stroke, seated herself on the rude chair of honor. After a second, she stood up again and called the meeting to order.

Under Gan's ruthless eyes, the trial was repeated, almost word for word, and the vote taken. No one man was surprised that the verdict was found to be unanimously in favor of the barter agreement, whereby the Matriarchy would give Tor Branthak the secret of their longevity for his removal of troops.

THE TRIAL and vote were quite over, and everyone was standing about wondering apprehensively what next, when the *Warspear* loomed hugely down from overhead, settling on a pillar of flame, landing among the huge trees rather neatly. Instantly out of the ship poured Gan's crew—and Gan's description to little Elvir of what a pirate looked like was fulfilled, for they looked very bold and bad, and the blasters in their hands seemed very large indeed.

They quickly disarmed the warrior women, who could not bring themselves to begin firing in the mass of people present. Gan kept the deadly fission ring gun trained upon the group of officers who had gathered about the old leader. As soon as things looked safely in their hands, Gan gave orders to his mates.

"Take that group of females about the old hag, there, aboard the *Warspear*. Then scout around and pick yourselves wives; you'll never get a better chance. If they behave, they can make our dismal rock hangout into a home for us. I see no reason why we can't let Tor Branthak search for the secret in his own way, now that we have it. These women know what the secret is and how to use it, and we will have it merely by taking them with us."

In some twenty minutes they had secured nearly a hundred and fifty captives from among the most beautiful of the warrior maids, as well as the dozen sleek officers of the Amazon army who had clustered about their leader, and the old woman also.

Aphele went aboard willingly, while Celys and her two look-alikes, her daughter and granddaughter, had to be dragged aboard. Then the *Warspear* lifted into the sky and Gan set course for far space, where the lonely Black Rock circled about a dying sun.

CHAPTER THIRTEEN

IT WAS some months later when the *Warspear* reappeared over Phira. She did not land, but dropped off a life-raft, moved on out of vision.

Within the life-raft Gan and Chan DuChaile, as well as the old Matriarch who had ruled for so long from hidden Avalaon, drifted slowly to a landing upon the plateau above the city. There were still a score of Konaparian vessels cradled there, as well as fifty or more damaged vessels of Phira, which had been captured and brought in. The rest of Konapar's original war-fleet had returned home, or patrolled the skies above Phira for the chance of retaliation by some ally of Phira.

Gan and his two companions were led before Tor Branthak in his ship, in the same chamber where Gan had toasted the long life of the Phiran women.

"You traitor!" shouted Tor Branthak when he recognized the Cap. "You dare return here? I had thought you would have better sense than to put yourself in my hands again."

"Why not?" Gan said. "Wasn't that our bargain; that I would return with the secret? So, I have returned. I didn't say when, as it was a question only to be determined by events. Tell me, Tor Branthak, have you discovered the secret yet?"

Gan laughed, and after a moment the Regent laughed too. "Tell your tale, Captain. But I must warn you, for this length of time I have considered you a liar and a scoundrel who stole away with the greatest treasure on Phira."

Gan said: "No, Your Highness. I did not steal it. I needed this time to get to the bottom of their secret. I abducted the core personnel and their leader because I believed there is only one way to get the secret—your tactics of pulling out their toenails seemed too drastic, and less liable to work than mine."

"And what is your method?"

Gan drew himself up to his full height, demonstrating the magnificent manhood in him. "Your Highness, when a human being has been without a vital element of life for a thousand years, that element should prove to be a very potent persuasive force. Besides, it has the advantage of not killing or maiming them."

The Tor grimaced at him. "Had you left me *any* core personnel at all, Captain Gan Alain, perhaps I *too* might have had the means to learn the secret. But, go on, our bargain still holds."

Gan pointed to the old lady. "I have brought her to you. She knows the secret of their long life, and will give it to you, in return for consent to return Phira to the rule of women."

Tor Branthak scowled. "A hard bargain, that, but the method might be worth it. But how explain to the men who have fought and been wounded, who have settled here on lands deeded to them? How can I give it back?"

Gan shrugged. "That is *her* price. I promised to bring her here and present it. But, if you want *my* price, I can offer you an alternative. I have learned the details of their methods, a rather simple preparation of certain reagents, which eliminate the substances that cause old age from the body, thus insuring perpetual youth. I will settle for a governorship on Phira, under your suzerainty, because I think you are a man's man, so that Phira would become in effect a province of Konapar, with me as its head. I have an itch to teach these Matriarchs something about the rights of the human male."

As Gan delivered these words, the old Matriarch turned on him with a sudden fierce exclamation, as if a serpent had bitten her. She flashed a knife from her full bosom, sprang upon Gan. The knife plunged into his chest. But the point turned on the heavy leather of his corselet, and he caught her wrist, twisted until her hand released the blade.

The Tor's eyes gleamed. "I understand your itch, exactly, Captain Gan Alain. Or, as I should say, from now on, Governor Gan Alain!"

Gan whipped up the Matriarch's knife and lifted it in salute. "To my Regent's long life!" he bellowed.

SO ENDED the ancient dominance of the female on Phira; and later, on the other worlds, which had come under the sway of the Matriarchs of Myrmi-Atla. But, as can be seen, if it had not been for Gan Alain and his *Warspear*, the fleet of Konapar would have been driven back by the dreadnought of Mixar, and with their monopoly of the *secret*, the Matriarchy would have grown in time to engulf all mankind.

Today, centuries after, the methods for fighting age developed by the Matriarchs have become the common property throughout the civilized portions of the galaxy. And on Phira, the harem of the mighty Gan Alain, Governor of Phira, in Alid, is the most famous for its beauty and talent of any in all the polygamous worlds.

The favorite of the Governor's harem is a very lovely brunette named Aphele, but the three identical beauties, Celys

I, II and III are more celebrated. The woman called Elvir is also much spoken of, because of her pranks and her mischievous beauty; and so too is a slim young beauty who still remembers her first kiss, and gets as much of a kick out of each succeeding one.

And the children of Gan Alain number seven hundred and ten.

THE END

CITIES VAPORIZED ACROSS AMERICA

The Communists had finally made their big move. Unfortunately, it was the big "nuclear" move. Stark terror and total devastation enveloped the face of the planet. Who would save humanity when the trusted leaders of government could no longer be trusted?

In this riveting portrayal of the horrors of nuclear war, veteran science fiction author Irving Cox shows us that it's the "little" people who will likely survive the horrors of nuclear war. Facing seemingly insurmountable odds, they band together in an effort to bring peace to a world in tatters—peace and a semblance of sanity to a devastated mankind. But while their intentions are noble, their chances of success seem decidedly low…

CAST OF CHARACTERS

JERRY BONHILL
A young idealist, a leader—with a big body and big fists. He is the new beginning in a world rocked by a nuclear holocaust.

CHERYL FINEBERG
She found a friend in Jerry, this fiery, strong-willed redhead. Along with the rest of her generation, she inherited chaos!

GEORGE KNIGHT
A gentle Quaker whose ideals were the centerpiece of his life. Was he prepared to give his life in defense of peace?

ANTON ZERGOFF
He was a beast with a man's body. He waded knee-deep in blood—but found no victory.

DR. STEWART ROSWELL
This brilliant educator stood face to face with the brutality he had previously only written of in his books.

BORIS YOROVICH
His strong principles gave him a change of heart about his role as an enemy invader.

WILLIE CLAPPER
This ex-minister was a traitor for profit. The Judas-Man who found contempt wherever he turned.

CHEN PHIANG
Haunted by the ghosts of his ancestors, this Red Chinese soldier could not remain an aggressor.

ONE OF OUR CITIES IS MISSING

By
IRVING COX

ARMCHAIR FICTION & MUSIC
PO Box 4369, Medford, Oregon 97504

Part One

The First Twelve Hours

I. The City—Thursday, 6:50 P.M. Dr. Stewart Roswell

THERE were no crowds in the churches, no mobs in the bars. People did what they always had. It was an amazing strength of mind or a terrifying blindness: I didn't know which.

Half an hour before the broadcast, I drove downtown. I parked my car and walked toward the big hotel on the beach. Two women came out of a beauty parlor; I heard one of them whisper, "They say Dr. Clapper took off for the hills early this afternoon. He has a cabin up there, stocked with enough food to last him ten years."

On the terrace of the hotel I stopped to light a cigarette, shielding my face from the cold sea wind. The sun flamed red on the Pacific horizon. In the harbor I saw the dark silhouettes of freighters at anchor. At noon the navy had sailed for Hawaii.

A girl, as dream-like as the yellow organdy she was wearing, sat alone on a stone bench at the far end of the terrace. She was twenty, perhaps. Black hair framed her face like an ivory cameo. Her lips were very red, her eyes large and dark, her cheeks cold marble.

"I shouldn't have come," she said, smiling at me. "I wanted—I wanted something; it isn't here."

"My dear, no one can live a lifetime in an hour."

"The truth is, I was afraid."

"We all are tonight."

"I thought it would be easier if I could be where there

were other people. It doesn't help."

I tossed my cigarette over the railing and sat on the bench beside her. "There's nothing to be afraid of yet. Perhaps they've found a way to work it out."

"Not this time; they can't."

"They always have before." I glanced at my watch. "It's almost time for the broadcast."

She put her hand on mine. It was long and graceful, as cold as alabaster. "Wait a little longer, please; I can't go back in there yet. I felt as if the walls were closing in on me, choking me; that's why I came out here—" She was suddenly shy, like a small child. "But I shouldn't be talking to you like this. I don't even know your name."

"Dr. Stewart Roswell," I told her. "I teach history at the State College."

"*The* Stewart Roswell? I've read your books."

That surprised me. My half-dozen books, warmly reviewed in the scholarly publications, gave me prestige but skimpy royalties. They were not what a young girl would pick up for light reading. The style was pedantic; the theme, international relations.

"I'm Maria D'Orlez." She held my hand gravely. "I was going to enroll at State next fall, Dr. Roswell. I counted on taking your classes."

Inside the hotel the throb of the dance orchestra stopped. I heard the sharp static of a public address system and the muffled voice of a radio announcer.

"The broadcast is beginning, Maria."

"Don't go in!" She drew me down on the stone bench. "We know what he's going to say—what he has to say."

For a time we sat together in silence. The girl was tense and her body trembled. I heard no sound but the muffled voice of the broadcast and, farther away, the rhythmic washing of waves on the beach. Even the traffic on the boulevard was still.

Suddenly people erupted from the hotel, running toward the street. Maria D'Orlez pulled me close.

"Stay with me," she whispered. "Stay with me."

II. The Highway—Thursday, 7:00 P.M. Jerry Bonhill

MOM stood in the doorway, twisting her hands in her apron. Dad sat on the couch, his face blank as if he were asleep with his eyes open. Mom gave him his usual glass of beer, but it stood untouched on the end table. We were watching the last part of "Doodle-Dan the Indian Man," kid stuff with a lot of old cartoons squeezed between the interminable commercials. But the program didn't matter. Not then.

Mom asked in a whisper, "Do you think he's worked something out?"

Dad shrugged and ran his hand through his gray hair. "We'll know in a few minutes, Abby."

I'm the baby in the Bonhill clan, nineteen last March. Dad sometimes calls me Postscript because I was born fifteen years after my sister Jane. I would have been in the army the way her husband Ronny was, but instead I joined the R. O. T. C. at the university.

"Doodle-Dan the Indian Man" ended with a trumpet fanfare. A flag came on the TV screen; we heard the national anthem. A network announcer said,

"We take you now to a government shelter somewhere near the nation's capital for this special report to the American people. Ladies and gentlemen, the President of the United States."

Visual static disturbed the image for a moment. Then

we saw the face of the President.

"Forty-eight hours ago," he said, with none of the usual boom you expect from a politician, "Enemy troops occupied Paris. The government of the United States submitted a formal protest to Moscow, which has been ignored. This afternoon the Soviets proposed a high-level diplomatic conference for the negotiation and readjustment of our differences. We have conferred before and the agreements have been subsequently violated by Soviet arms. We have lost Asia to Moscow at the conference table; we have lost Africa; one by one we have lost our allies in Europe, until today only England remains beyond the Iron Curtain.

"I speak tonight fully conscious of the unspeakable horror of atomic war. I give you my solemn assurance that your government has explored every honorable means for keeping the peace. If we are to survive as free men, we have no recourse left to us but war.

"Tonight I have asked Congress for a declaration of war—a holy war and a just war, to free the uncounted millions who are now enslaved by the Communist dictatorship. Many of you who are listening to me will die; many of our cities will be destroyed. But victory, when it is ours—"

The screen went suddenly dark. We heard another voice, a machine-gun burst of words.

"Red Alert, Pacific Coast. At five-fifty tonight enemy planes crossed the radar defense screen in Northern Canada. Estimated number, five thousand heavy bombers. Following this announcement, all television channels will go off the air. Tune to local radio stations for additional directions."

For more than a minute we sat looking blankly at the

screen. Mom clenched her fist against her mouth. Her shoulders were shaking. Dad got up and put his arm around her. Neither of them seemed to know what to do. I went to my room and brought out my portable. Only one Los Angeles station was still broadcasting. We were prepared for that. It was part of the C. D. plan, which had been discussed for weeks in all the papers.

As I tuned in, the announcer was repeating the Red Alert. He was choked off before he finished, and we heard a second voice, rasping and shrill with fear:

"The Civil Defense Organization orders the evacuation of Los Angeles. Use private vehicles as much as possible. Municipal buses will be available at terminal points. Speed is essential; the city must be cleared within four hours. Safe evacuation areas are designated as the Mojave or the Owens Valley."

The order was repeated over and over. I snapped off the radio to save the batteries.

In five minutes we were ready. I strapped our warmest clothes into a bundle and I scared up two flashlights. I crammed the medicines from the bathroom chest into a beach bag. I took an axe, a hammer, and a couple of screwdrivers, as well as my hunting rifle.

As Dad backed our car out of the drive, I saw cars leaving other houses along the street.

"They always told us the shelters would be safe," said Mom. "It's sabotage, Chris; I'm sure of it. Subversives took over the station and made that announcement, just to get everybody on the street when the bombers came."

Dad snapped on the car radio. "In that case, there should be a correction by this time." He tuned in the proper band, but all we heard was the same evacuation bulletin.

"Dr. Clapper said it would happen like this," Mom persisted, "if we kept coddling our subversives."

"Clapper!" Dad spat the word like profanity. "That's all we need right now—advice from that knuckle-headed half-wit."

Willie Clapper was Mom's knight in shining armor. Lots of people—women, particularly—fell for his line. He had once been a minister of a reputable church, but the congregation had kicked him out. Every Sunday, for more than five years, Willie Clapper had put on a half-hour TV network show; the time was paid for by an anonymous millionaire. Almost everybody made Clapper's subversive list: businessmen, professors, priests, writers.

Dad pulled the car to a stop when we were on the freeway and asked me to drive. "We have to make time, Jerry," he said. "You handle the car better than I do."

It was the first time he ever made that concession.

From time to time I snapped on the car radio. Once I picked up the whisper of a San Francisco station, but that was all. The San Francisco announcer was reading an official bulletin. The invading fleet was close to the U.S.-Canadian border, still flying high in the stratosphere. The Nike and interceptor fighters had brought down better than a third of the bombers, and the government was confident that none of the enemy ships would reach any important targets.

The bombers, which had fallen, carried H-bombs built to explode on contact. A gapping wound had been torn across the face of Canada; most of the peripheral defense positions were wiped out; fire on a fifteen-hundred-mile front swept the north woods. Scattered information from the surviving radar outposts reported a second enemy fleet had crossed the Arctic Circle shortly after seven o'clock.

"They're gambling everything," Dad said as the broadcast faded under a blanket of static, "on knocking us out with one sneak attack."

"Dr. Clapper warned us," Mom chimed in. "He said, if we didn't build our border defenses—"

"Damn it, Abby!" Dad raked his fingers through his hair. "This is real; this is for keeps! Can't you get that through your head?"

Mom and Dad always tore into each other when Willie Clapper's name came up. I was trying to think of a way to sidetrack the argument, when we heard the dull thunder of an explosion somewhere behind us.

Mom screamed. There were more explosions. Flashes of light, like heat lightning, flickered on the western horizon.

We were close to San Bernardino by that time. Both sides of the highway were crowded with cars, but we were moving at a good speed. The planes came suddenly, slashing out of the night sky.

Bullets splattered the cars. Somewhere ahead of us a gas tank exploded. I heard the terrified screams and the grinding of metal upon metal, as automobiles piled up on the road. The planes came again. Holes appeared in a diagonal line across our windshield. Mom cried out and covered her eyes. Dad slumped on the seat beside her.

I twisted the wheel desperately to miss the wreckage. The car banged through the guardrail into a ditch. It lurched sickeningly, and righted itself again. Dad slid off the seat.

The rear wheels spun in the mud, caught suddenly, and hurled the car into an orange grove beside the highway. I jammed down the brake as the front bumper came up against a tree trunk. My head snapped against the broken windshield. I blacked out.

I STOPPED a stranger as he left the hotel; he said the Civil Defense Organization had ordered the evacuation of Los Angeles. For years they had told us not to jam the highways during an emergency. This last minute change seemed pure hysteria, not good sense.

"Are you leaving, Dr. Roswell?" Maria D'Orlez asked.

"My dear child, I'm nearly sixty; at my age, a man doesn't start running for his life."

"You aren't afraid of the bomb?"

"I've learned to live with it."

"And the Russians: are you afraid of them?"

She asked the question seriously, her dark eyes large and intent. I tried to give her an honest, rational answer. "The Russian people are like other human beings; like ourselves. The tragedy of our time is that we were never able to find a basis for mutual understanding. The iron wall that separates us—"

"You wrote in one of your books, 'Common men in the Soviet world are no more aggressive or warlike, than the average American.' Do you still believe that, Dr. Roswell?"

It surprised me that she had the wording so accurately. "I was writing about the general traits common to all people," I explained, "not a form of government. Keep that in mind, Maria."

"Oh, I wasn't being critical!" Her eyes were wide with innocence. "I agree with you completely."

I looked at her sharply. I had a feeling she was mocking me. She slipped her hand into mine. "Will you drive me home, Dr. Roswell?"

When we got into my car, Maria moved very close to me. "I don't want to go home yet. I want to see what other people are doing."

"But your parents, Maria—"

She smiled mysteriously. "They'll understand."

We drove through areas where people were packing clothing and food in cars. I was surprised at the orderliness of the evacuation and absence of panic. You might have thought the people were all going on a mass picnic. They were cheerful, as if the whole thing was a lark; they called jokes back and forth; they were helping each other.

Maria D'Orlez seemed disturbed; certainly not pleased. A dark shadow of anger crossed her face.

"I'd better take you home now," I said when we returned to the car.

"Not yet." She glanced at a clock on a public building; the hands stood at eight-ten. "Let's go up on the hill, Dr. Roswell, and look down at the city—one more look at the bright lights before they're gone."

It was after nine when I parked at the viewpoint on the crest of the hill. The night was unusually clear. The lighted city streets spread out below us in a geometric checkerboard. We could see the endless columns of headlights moving away from the city on the freeways— like an army of marching fireflies.

"Americans are gilt-edged fools," Maria said suddenly. "They'll lose this war, but there was a time once when they could have wiped out the Reds—when they had weapons the Russians couldn't match."

"Not fools, Maria; humanitarians. We put our faith in justice instead of brute force."

"Force is justice, Dr. Roswell. To win: that's the only thing that counts."

"And you believe they will?"

"The Communists have planned this for a long time;

they've calculated all the risks. Tonight the strength is on their side, and they won't be afraid to use it."

"Only material power, Maria. There's something else—"

She laughed.

A blast of fire and flame shot up from the entrance through the harbor breakwater, followed rapidly by a dozen more explosions. Something—enemy submarines?—had triggered the mines protecting the harbor. Cold fear rose in my throat. Maria looked at her watch, and flung her arms around my neck.

"I'm frightened—terribly frightened," she whispered. I felt her lips warm on mine, her fingers tearing, like cat claws, at the back of my skull.

There were more explosions in the harbor. Debris fountained up from the navy installations. Enemy submarines were there; that much was clear. A suicide squad had come first, exploding the mines; the rest were pouring through the gap.

I tried to pull Maria's hands away from my neck. I felt the pinprick of the needle and I heard her say,

"We still have a use for you intellectuals, Dr. Roswell—for a while yet."

I wanted to push her from me. I wanted to fling myself out of the car. But my body went limp and a black nightmare closed over my mind. The last thing I saw was the Madonna smile on Maria's face, lit by the scarlet fire of the explosions in the harbor.

IV. The Highway—Thursday 11:00 P.M. Jerry Bonhill

"JERRY! JERRY, your father's dead!" The shrill scream came from far away. I felt cold hands pulling at my shirt, dragging me back from the emptiness. Pain throbbed in my head. I opened my eyes.

I couldn't have been out for more than a minute. The planes were still diving at the highway, slashing bullets into the shambles. All the traffic had stopped, held up by the wreckage.

People were running from their cars and leaping into the ditch. A poor concealment, for the gasoline left no sheltering darkness. The planes came again, firing into the ditch. I could hear the cries of the dying and the wounded, above the jet-blast of the motors.

Mom helped me out of the car. With her handkerchief she dabbed at the cut on my forehead, where my head had struck the windshield. When I heard the swelling roar of the planes a third time, I jerked Mom down on the earth. We rolled beneath the car. A bullet hit one of the windows and the fragmented glass clattered against the open door.

In five minutes it was over: that first taste of hell. Flights of planes came out of the east, with wing-mounted guns blasting at the enemy. The air battle joined high above us. We heard the angry clatter of machine guns and the roar of motors. Sometimes a plane fell, making a comet-trail of fire in the night sky.

Men were hauling the wreckage off the highway. I joined them. In ten minutes we had one lane clear. The refugee cars began to move again.

We were still clearing the highway when the Red Cross helicopters came, settling into the field beyond the grove. Army Medical Corpsmen lifted the seriously wounded into stretchers and loaded them in the waiting ships. One of the pilots told me the unit came from March Field. He gestured toward the air battle thundering overhead.

"They're our boys up there, what's left of them. They must have tangled with the whole, damn Red air force."

"What's happening?" I asked.

"This is one of the neatest sneak attacks on record." He fumbled in his jacket pocket for a cigarette. "First they fouled up the roads so we can't get any transports to go through, and then—"

"You mean the evacuation of L. A.? It was on the radio. I heard it myself."

"Half a dozen sympathizers, could hold a station long enough to make the announcement. Afterward they wrecked every transmitter in the city, so the C. D. couldn't broadcast a correction. That's the way we have it doped out."

"But the Russian planes—"

"A couple of hours after the highways were nicely jammed, Red subs broke through into the Los Angeles harbor. We don't know how many—none of our boys have got close enough to see—but it's a damn big chunk of their fleet. The subs launched the fighter planes, and they're probably putting men ashore by this time. They've bought themselves a beachhead, unless we can move transports down these roads mighty quick."

"Don't we have any bases closer to the city?"

"The Soviets have given us the works—everything in one knockout attack. Most of our fighter planes were shuttled north to intercept the big bombers. This L. A. landing has us where the hair is short. All we have at March Field are the cadets, still in flight school."

"And the navy?" I asked.

"Most of the Pacific Fleet is at Hawaii—that is, the ships the Red subs haven't sunk. The Reds will probably hold their beachhead for a while. But if they want to exploit it, they're going to need a hell of a lot of manpower. How will they get it here? Tonight they're throwing away their air force and a big piece of their submarine fleet. And don't forget: no Soviet city is going to survive our H-- bombs. We aren't licked yet, kid; not by a long shot."

There were only four people still in the grove—Mom, a leather-faced old man, a girl of about my age, and a small boy of nine. And, of course, the dead, laid out in rows under the trees.

The three people were strays Mom had taken under her wing. It was a habit of hers. The man said his name was Pat Thatcher. He had lost his car in the pile-up.

The child was Jim Riley. His parents had been killed in the strafing. We knew nothing about the girl. She sat motionless, in a state of shock. She had been like that when they pulled her out of the shambles. She wasn't beautiful, but she was well put together. Red hair cut short, like a boy's; blue eyes; a tiny, turned-up nose; and freckles on her cheeks.

I examined the car. Except for the broken windshield and side window, it seemed undamaged. But the wheels were bogged deep in the soft soil. With Pat Thatcher's help I dug out the back wheels and began to push the car toward solid ground.

Little Jim Riley and the redheaded girl squeezed in the back beside our cartons of canned food and the bundles of clothing.

Mom and Thatcher sat in front with me. I started the motor and put the car in gear. That was my first indication that we had anything wrong. The engine pounded as if it had a bad case of mechanical asthma; the front wheels shimmied on the highway.

"You'll have to fix it," Mom shouted.

"Nothing he can do," Thatcher replied.

The shimmy of the front wheels became steadily worse. After we started up the grade, it was impossible to push the car any faster than fifteen miles an hour. It was midnight before we reached the three-thousand-foot level.

I tried the car radio again. I couldn't raise San Francisco, but I brought in the faint, fading signal of another station—probably Salt Lake City. The announcer was saying,

"…first rumor of a Soviet landing at Los Angeles, and the government spokesman declared the rumor was without foundation. In a second bulletin…" Static for half a minute. The radio came up loud again, "…the bombing of Boston and Tacoma. There is as yet no reliable estimate of casualties in Detroit and Chicago; both cities were partially evacuated before the H-bombs fell. Our only news out of Europe is still three hours old. During the first twenty minutes of the war, Soviet planes dropped H-bombs on the major English cities; the British had insufficient time to carry out any effective evacuation of their larger centers of population. British heavy bombers made retaliatory raids on the continent, but we still have no confirmation…"

The voice was choked out by static. We couldn't bring in the station again; I snapped off the radio. Mom began to twist her hands together, frowning uncertainly.

"Jerry," she asked, "does that mean England's fighting on our side?"

"It's their war, too, Mom, just as much as it's ours."

"But Dr. Clapper always said they wouldn't—they wanted to knife us in the back. I'm—I'm actually glad Dr. Clapper was wrong for once." Her lips began to tremble; I saw tears on her cheeks. She added, wistfully, "I wish I could have made myself say that while Chris was still alive."

The car wheezed past the four-thousand-foot marker.

Suddenly a flash of white lit the northern sky, beyond the ridge of the mountain. Two or three seconds passed. Waves of concussion bent the tops of the pines, like a storm wind; a thunder of sound shook the earth. Jim Riley awoke and started to cry.

"The H-bomb!" Mom gasped.

"No farther north than Santa Barbara," Thatcher added. "That's my guess."

Then we heard the roar of big bombers, growing louder and louder in the night sky. I saw them in the moonlight. Not one or two, but scores. They swept low over the city. Tiny figures dropped in rhythmic precision toward the earth. In a moment thousands of dark-colored parachutes ballooned in the air.

V. The City—Thursday, Midnight Dr. Stewart Roswell

I RECOVERED slowly from the opiate Maria D'Orlez had given me. I saw her behind the wheel of my car. The dashlight reflected upward gave her face a saintly expression—the Madonna mask.

Slowly I pushed myself up on the seat beside her. I hadn't the strength to do anything else. My mind was in a stupor.

Maria turned south on the oceanfront boulevard, high on the bluff above the beach. The moving panel of moonlight on the water passed across the submarines surfaced in the harbor. I saw the catapults launching the fighter planes, and the crowded landing barges moving toward the shore.

"I'm sorry, Dr. Roswell," Maria said suddenly, in a sultry voice.

"You help to betray your own country—" My voice was high-pitched, unrecognizable, the voice of a stranger. "—and that's all you can say?"

"We need spokesmen, respectable men to explain our position to the American people."

"And you honestly believe you can force me to spread Communist propaganda?"

"Truth, Dr. Roswell. You and the others. You were my assignment tonight. I followed your car when you went downtown; that's how I met you at the hotel."

"But force, Maria—"

"Education." That one word was crisp and granite-hard. "When your mind is washed clean of all the bourgeois rubbish you've been taught to believe, you'll know how to speak for the people. It is a great awakening, Dr. Roswell, a wonderful awakening to a glorious, new world."

She brought my car to a stop in front of a large mansion on the oceanfront, one of the gaudiest, pseudo-Spanish

cathedrals of Millionaire's Row. I was still too weak to stand alone; Maria had to help me up the brick walk.

I recognized the house. It belonged to Marvin Harlip Dragen III, the addle-witted fourth-generation heir of a nineteenth century robber baron who spent a good part of his life dabbling at matrimony. What time and energy he had left over he devoted to Causes. He was in the strangely inconsistent position of controlling an enormous fortune, while at the same time loudly condemning the means by which it had been acquired. He was the angel of American Communism.

"You've brought us another guest, Miss D'Orlez!" He beamed. "How delightful."

"Dr. Stewart Roswell," she said.

"The historian? We are pleased to have you join us, Comrade Roswell." Dragen rubbed his hands together. "It goes straight to the heart, doesn't it?—so many prominent men volunteering their help."

"Where's his room, Marvin?"

"Yes, a room—of course." Dragen took a list from his pocket and studied it carefully. He was a little, soft man. His round face rode above rolls of fat. His eyes were small, dark, agate beads set too close together in a wad of pink clay. His yellow hair was plastered back on his skull to hide the balding crown. The unreal coloring of his cheeks, the bright slash of his mouth, obviously cried his use of cosmetics. "We still have one empty room for Dr. Roswell—third floor, on the corner. Though I'm afraid we'll have to start doubling up when our other friends arrive."

Marvin rang a bell. Two strong-arm boys, armed with pistols, came from a side room and pushed me roughly toward the stairway. Still unsteady on my feet, I stumbled and fell. Grinning, one of the men kicked me viciously in the groin. I lay against the steps, paralyzed by pain.

Dragen waddled toward me, fluttering his pudgy hands. "I do hope you aren't hurt, Dr. Roswell. It was an accident; you understand that, naturally. These Comrades are really as gentle as doves. They save their anger for the enemies of the people."

Maria D'Orlez said, without feeling, "I'm sure Dr. Roswell doesn't want to be an enemy of the people."

"A bloated plutocrat," Dragen added.

"But he may require a little education…" Maria's voice trailed away in a frightening silence.

The strong-arm boys laughed and jerked me to my feet. They dragged me up three flights of steps, pushed open a bedroom door and flung me into the room. I heard the key turn in the lock. I lay on the floor, aware of nothing but pain. I felt myself retching. I tried to crawl away. My hand touched the leg of a chair. Slowly I pulled myself up until I could rest against the chair. After a time the pain subsided.

The door key grated in the lock. I swung around, instinctively afraid. (Had I learned my first lesson, then, so soon ?—to respond to every new stimulus with fear?) I expected Dragen's bullyboys; but it was Maria D'Orlez. She slid into the room stealthily, pressing her finger on her lips.

She handed me a small glass containing a milky liquid. "I know what Dragen's men did. Drink this, Dr. Roswell. It will take away the pain."

I pushed the glass away. "Or drug me again."

"Don't say that. I can't stand that look of accusation in your eyes. I want to help you."

"Is that why you brought me here?"

"We must have you on our side, Dr. Roswell. We need men of your intelligence and ability."

"Possibly, when your goons finish what you call education—"

"But you don't have to go through that." She put the glass on the dresser and came closer to me. I smelled the gardenia scent of her hair and, even in the darkness, I saw her fragile, Madonna smile. "That's why I had to risk talking to you again. The others don't know I'm here. You must never tell them." She put her hand unexpectedly on mine. "Or may I—may I call you Stewart?"

Her air of timid conspiracy was contrived. I knew how they operated: first the mailed fist, then soft words—any device that won their dialectic objective.

"Please, Stewart, forget your bitterness." Her tears were surprisingly real. "It's true I forced you to come here; that was my assignment. But I sincerely admire your books; the whole party does. In spirit you've always been one of us.

We ask only peace and freedom for all humanity, an international democracy of goodwill and brotherhood."

"Word games, Maria."

She drew away from me and her face became cold marble. "All right, Stewart. Let's forget that—junk your idealism—and talk about practical things. You want to save your own neck; every man does. When the Soviets win this war—"

"You seem sure of that, Maria. Why?"

"Because we put our bets on material reality, the logistics of weapons. We're not waiting for any vague spiritual nonsense to work a miracle for us. Tonight, Stewart, Soviet H-bombs will wipe out nearly every industrial city in the United States. Except one."

"You think the Russian cities are immune?"

She shrugged. "They're part of the gamble."

"And the people who die?"

"Martyrs in our great crusade for peace. We'll build them a fine memorial in the new Moscow." She gestured toward the harbor, where the explosions were becoming less frequent. "This is what counts, Stewart; this one industrial center which is going to survive. Four hundred of the bombers in the second wave that crossed Canada tonight are carrying paratroops—not bombs. The issue is being settled here, Stewart. By midnight we'll have our beachhead in America: a harbor for our submarines, refineries to turn out fuel, heavy industry still undamaged. With Los Angeles as our base of operations, what problem will we have conquering a nation already in chaos from the bombing? America will surrender within a week."

Maria D'Orlez was no longer an enigma, but a tragic symbol of our failure to achieve our own ideals.

For myself, I knew the choice was very close. The

strong-arm boys would be back to resume the farce they called education. Did I have the guts to hold to what I believed? Did I have the faith and the conviction of the Christian martyr?—for only that could overturn the empire of the Politburo.

VI. The Ridge—Friday morning, 12:30 A.M. Jerry Bonhill

JIM RILEY was still crying. Mom reached over the seat and tried to comfort him. I felt her body stiffen. "Jerry!" she gasped. "The girl…"

In the rearview mirror I saw the redhead kneeling on the seat and aiming my rifle at the planes overhead. She pulled the trigger again and again, while the hammer clicked against the empty chamber.

"Let her be," Pat Thatcher told us. "It may bring her out of the shock."

We were at the top of the hill, close to the mountain village of Running Springs. It was not a large village. Half a dozen stores, a tavern, and a tourist lodge. In the hills back of the highway were a number of vacation cabins. I banged on the door of the general store, which was also the post office and service station. When I had no answer, I tried the other stores before I crossed the highway to the tavern. A note, hastily block-printed, fluttered from the door.

"Running Springs and Arrowhead evacuated. Inquire at Victorville."

I walked back to the car. The red-haired girl was crying softly. Her logjam of emotion had been broken. I told Thatcher Running Springs had been evacuated. He got out and looked thoughtfully at the gasoline pump in front of the general store; then he broke the lock and pushed the hose nozzle into our tank.

Thatcher and I got back into the car. The girl was no longer crying. Mom still sat beside her, caressing her hand; Jim moved into the front seat, between Thatcher and me.

"I—I want to thank you," the girl said, "for taking care of me." She bit her lip to hold back her tears. "I'm Cheryl Fineberg. If we could get through to our house at Palm Springs, we would be able to stay there. We've plenty of food and—and—"

"Your father was the movie producer?" Thatcher asked.

"Yes. I saw him die. And mother—she threw herself in front of me. She was trying to say something. I saw her lips open. Then—then blood came from her mouth. And father slumped down and the car rammed into something." She clenched her fists over her eyes.

"Don't think about it," Mom said. "We all lost someone back there."

"I won't give in to it again," the girl promised.

I put the car in gear and we wobbled out of Running Springs, driving east toward Big Bear Lake.

"Jerry," Mom said. "I just happened to remember: Dr. Clapper has a mountain cabin somewhere near here— between Running Spring and Snow Valley."

Thatcher put in, "Clapper took off for the hills before noon; I picked up the rumor somewhere."

"Jerry, if we could find him," Mom proposed eagerly, "I'm sure he'd put us up for a while."

"I'd rather take a chance on the Commies," Thatcher answered.

Jim Riley spoke up, "I'm sure I smell smoke!"

So did I. Half a minute later, as we swung around a granite shelf towering over the road, we saw the wall of fire lapping at the pines a mile or so north of the highway.

"We can't go back," Thatcher snapped. "We'll have to outrun it."

"In this junk heap?" I asked.

I pushed the car faster than I should. Once or twice, on a sharp curve, the shimmying wheels almost sent us off the bank. Yet I didn't seem to be able to increase the safety margin between the fire and us. If anything, the smoke in the air was getting thicker. The billowing white blanket blotted out the moonlight. The haze and the darkness reduced our visibility to less than ten feet.

A big buck darted suddenly in front of us. I had no time to jam on the brakes. We hit him. The body jolted under the wheels. I heard the sharp snap of metal; the wheel spun in my hand; and the car lurched out of control into the embankment.

Thatcher leaped out and looked beneath the car. He straightened slowly. "Well, that finishes the axle; we start walking now."

"What about our food?" Mom demanded. "And our clothes—"

"We'll take everything we can carry. Jerry, do you know where we are?"

"We just passed Snow Valley. It isn't much more than a mile to Lakeview Point, at the top of the grade."

"We may be all right on the other side. A firebreak runs along the ridge; if the wind's right, there's a good chance the fire won't cross it."

Mom and Cheryl Fineberg took the bundles of clothing, which were lighter. Thatcher and I carried the cartons of canned goods. Jim Riley insisted on doing his part, so we gave him the water thermos. I've handled a fifty-pound pack on camping trips and it never bothered me.

We made very slow progress. When we heard the

crackling of the fire somewhere behind us, I was ready to drop the boxes and make a run for it. But Pat Thatcher trudged on without looking back and his courage influenced the rest of us.

The air sucked in by the heat dispersed the smoke. The moon was clear above us again. Looking back, I saw that the fire had not yet crossed the highway. Then, above the roar of flames, I heard the purr of a motor.

"Someone's coming!" Mom cried. "He'll pick us up and get us out of this."

Thatcher said doubtfully, "When it's every man for himself—"

We moved to the shoulder of the road as a blue Cadillac swung around the curve. In the red light of the fire, we all saw the driver clearly. A big man, as sleekly handsome as his car, dark-haired and bushy-browed: the somber face we had all seen so often on the TV screen.

"Dr. Clapper," Mom said, with a sigh of relief. "Thank God. He'll help us."

She stepped out on the road, waving her arms. It was obvious that Willie Clapper saw her. His face was suddenly torn with a terrible fear. He gunned the motor and almost ran Mom down as he swung past us. A hundred yards beyond, he stopped long enough to throw something out of the car. It burst into flame and the fire fed along the dry carpet of pine needles. We began to run, but long before we reached the spot the brush had caught and the fire was across the highway. Behind us the inferno broke out again and we were trapped in a closing ring of flame. The sound of Clapper's car receded in the distance.

Mom stood on the road, the flickering flame throwing distorted shadows on her face. "Dr. Clapper did that," she said. "He did it deliberately—Dr. Clapper!"

Thatcher said, "When a man panics—"

"But he wasn't frightened until he saw us!"

Thatcher motioned toward a bluff of bare gravel rising beyond the highway. "We might still pull through if we get under there. Nothing within fifty feet of it will burn."

We dropped our cartons and slid down the embankment. We had to cross a deep gully. A tiny stream trickled over the rocks. The water was hot, coated with a scum of carbon particles.

It was the gully that saved us. We were still at the bottom, sheltered by a block of granite eight feet high, when the sky above the fire blazed white.

"They've dropped an H-bomb on the desert."

I heard Thatcher say that in the split-second before the chaos tore loose around us. The earth shook. The bare bluff where we had meant to take refuge came apart and the ground lashed toward us like a wave of muddy water. Instinctively we fell flat in the stream, sheltered by the pile of granite. I felt the water flowing hot against my chest. I heard Mom scream.

The hurricane of loose earth lashed over us. I felt tiny stones cut across my back. A tree fell over the gully, hung there for a moment, and was whipped away again.

Suddenly it was over.

None of us was seriously hurt, although in places our skin had been rubbed raw by the abrasive force of flying soil. I stood up. The air was filled with fine dust. The bluff of bare earth was gone.

But the blast of flying gravel had turned the front of the fire. The road to the crest was open.

AN HOUR or more after Maria D'Orlez left my room the door was thrown open again. Marvin Dragen III stood on the threshold, kneading his fat hands together. His two strong-arm boys flung a stranger on the floor. The man—slightly built, graying, wearing a dark business suit—was unconscious, his face badly beaten, his white shirt spotted with blood.

"I'm afraid I must impose on you, Dr. Roswell," Dragen smirked, licking his painted lips. "We have so many guests. I'll have to ask you to share your room. You and Comrade Knight—" He indicated the unconscious man. "—will enjoy having a little chat."

When they were gone, I lifted Knight into the chair. With my handkerchief I wiped the blood away from his lips. Still unconscious, he muttered in a hoarse, almost incomprehensible whisper, "Turn the other cheek...the other cheek..." His name sounded familiar, and I might have recognized him if his face had not been distorted by welts and bruises.

At last he opened his eyes. For a split-second I saw fear; then, a quiet composure. "Dr. Roswell!" His voice was low-pitched and gentle, with a faint undertone of a New England accent. "I didn't know you were one of them."

"I'm a prisoner just as you are."

The grimace behind the bruises was meant to be a smile. "They expected me to demonstrate how to turn the other cheek. I'm a Quaker, you see. Religious pacifism seems to be particularly obnoxious to them."

George Knight, the Quaker: I knew him then. I had met him once or twice at educational meetings. He had been a banker and later a college president; five years ago he resigned in order to give his full time to the work of the American Friends Service Committee.

"They sent a young man to bring me in," George Knight said. "A university student. He had visited the Service Committee once."

"It still isn't clear to me what they want us to do."

"They aren't sure themselves. They're waiting for a boss of some sort who's on his way from Moscow to direct the occupation. The general idea is to use us in propaganda broadcasts. My young man showed me the list of names of the men they have imprisoned here tonight. Twenty-five of us, handpicked by Moscow; we each have an unusual prominence with special groups."

George Knight went on to name them all. I recognized the names; a few of the men I knew personally. Writers, lecturers, priests, a financier, two industrialists whose farsighted labor policies had set a pattern for business, a judge, a newspaper editor, a Senator.

"All twenty-five of us have one thing in common," I told Knight. "We've been Willie Clapper's whipping boys."

"I hadn't thought of that. Actually, it was his telecasts that gave us the notoriety we have."

"And built up the special groups that give such weight to our opinions," I added. "An interesting coincidence."

"You aren't seriously suggesting —but that's preposterous!"

"Is it? Clapper took each of us out of relative obscurity and made our names familiar to a national audience. And we all live in the Los Angeles area, where they could round us up quickly. Why didn't Clapper dig out any pseudo-subversives anywhere else in the country?"

"But he must have—"

"Name one. In fact, Knight, name anyone Clapper attacked who isn't here tonight."

"Your argument can't hold water. Willard Clapper's accusations will nullify anything we broadcast. That wouldn't make sense, if he had been part of their conspiracy."

"The Reds can work around that —if they have Clapper here, too."

"I saw the list. His name wasn't there."

"He could come in of his own accord."

Far away I heard the sound of an automobile motor. It seemed ominous; the city had been quiet too long. I walked to the window. I saw the open car racing down the boulevard. With screaming brakes it stopped in front of the Dragen mansion. The driver sprang out and saluted, while a tall, uniformed man marched smartly up the walk, followed by four Soviet soldiers armed with submachine guns.

"I think the Moscow brass has arrived," I said to Knight. He looked at me, with a strangely intent light blazing in his eyes. Very quietly he answered,

"It will be Gordov."

"Who's Gordov?"

"A Soviet general—also one of the top men in the secret police."

"The university student told you? But what difference it makes—"

"A great deal. No one told me who was coming; I don't think they knew. You could say this answers a prayer of mine. If you prefer a more prosaic explanation, say I'm risking a guess on a good probability. Alex Gordov is one of the half-dozen men the Politburo was likely to consider for this job."

"You know Gordov, Knight?"

"I did, long ago. I've watched him climb to the top, over the wrecked careers—and sometimes the broken bodies—of his friends. He learned how to develop those traits so essential to the successful Soviet Man. When I met him, at a hospital in Leningrad, he was a youngster of sixteen—talented, a brilliant mind, far too sensitive for the Soviet pattern. He was a lieutenant in the infantry—at sixteen, badly wounded during the last days of the war. Our penicillin saved his arm from amputation. Gordov was very much aware of that, and it disturbed him a great deal because it didn't jibe with the American stereotype he had been taught. At the whim of some party functionary, Alex had been ordered to study English while he was in the hospital. He talked to me whenever he could— theoretically to improve his skill with the language — actually, because he was trying to find out what made me tick."

"It must have taken a weird twist of dialectic," I suggested, "for him to fit a Quaker into their version of our society."

"Alex had the intelligence to see reality beyond the fancy doubletalk of their party propaganda. He knew aggression for what it was, whether they called it peace or liberation. And he had an amazing capacity for love—in the abstract, Dr. Roswell: love for his fellow man —always anathema to the party. It was that, ultimately, which broke him to the Soviet machine. They did it quite simply. The usual technique: they had a use for Gordov, and they took him over in much the same way they did us tonight.

"His mother and sister had been arrested as enemies of the people. The secret police arranged for Alex to discover the name of the agent who was responsible. They allowed Gordov to take his revenge. Then he was arrested. The police showed him their file—enough evidence to condemn him to the firing squad. They made the usual offer. Gordov would go free if he agreed to work for them. They threw in freedom for his mother and sister as an added incentive.

"Alex learned his lesson and he learned it well. Since then he has climbed high, using the same methods of treachery and betrayal. But locked somewhere in his soul, Dr. Roswell, is the boy I knew—his capacity for love; his clear-eyed vision of the truth. I'm counting on that tonight."

"But what do you expect to do? What possible influence—"

"I shall be myself—the man Gordov remembers. I know it won't be easy. Alex may have to destroy me; as a matter of fact, I believe he will have no other choice. But, whatever happens, it will awaken the memory of the boy in his soul, it will arouse an inner conflict of the mind that only—"

Just then Dragon waddled into the room, followed by his two armed guards.

"Comrades, I have exciting news," he said. "The Comrade General from Moscow is eager to meet my guests. If you would be kind enough to come along with me—" He paused, frowning and fingering his lower lip. "But we do want to make a good impression, now, don't we? The Comrade General mustn't think we have bourgeois notions of class superiority."

He moved toward Knight and ripped off the Quaker's tie. When Knight moved back involuntarily, the guards snapped out their guns. "I expect your complete co-operation," Dragen remarked petulantly. "Stand at attention, please, Comrade Knight."

Knight and I were pushed into the hall. They took us downstairs into the living room.

Four Soviet soldiers, armed with submachine guns, lounged against an ornate table. Dragen and his two guards left the room again. One by one they assembled their twenty-five prisoners.

Dragen was reciting the familiar Communist cliches when the Soviet General entered from the hall. He was a tall, powerful, swarthy man; brooding intelligence—the crafty wit of expediency—flashed from his eyes, but his face was an impassive mask. A single medal swung from his tunic, the Order of Lenin. He had a bottle of vodka in his hand and from time to time he drank from it liberally.

And this, I thought, was Alex Gordov? This was the man George Knight hoped to move by the simple sincerity of his Quaker faith?

The General paused at the door, speaking crisply in good English almost without an accent to someone beyond my line of vision. "It's up to you to locate him," the General said. "Get him here; we don't accept excuses. At noon, I want to put this circus of intellectuals on the air."

Dragen had broken off his tirade when he saw the General. He made an ingratiating gesture and spoke to us in a fawning whisper. "Comrades, may I present your commanding officer—General Anton Zergoff."

I risked a glance in Knight's direction. I saw that his face had gone white; his lips were moving silently.

Zergoff took a pull at his bottle. He walked slowly along the lineup of prisoners. "I'm afraid I disappoint you—one of you, at least," he announced in a hoarse, parade ground bark. "Let me set your minds at ease immediately. General Gordov has been—" A slight pause for effect. "—taken care of. He expressed a reluctance to command the occupation when he saw the list of intellectuals we planned to recruit. Before his execution, General Gordov was persuaded to make a full confession. He has been an enemy of the people for years—since he was sixteen. One man was responsible, one of you—one man who had the power to reach into the highest ranks of the people's government and force a Soviet General to betray the revolution."

Anton Zergoff turned to face us, his feet spread wide, his face savage with rage. "Now it is my privilege to meet this pig—this stinking agent of capitalism; I shall personally supervise his re-education. Where is the Quaker who calls himself George Knight?"

Unhesitatingly Knight moved out of the rank of prisoners. There was a gentle smile on his battered face. He said softly, but in a voice we all could hear,

"So Alex remembered, God works His will in strange ways."

VIII. The Ridge—Friday, midnight until dawn. Jerry Bonhill

I HAD an uneasy feeling that Thatcher wasn't simply the ordinary old man he pretended. He spoke too well, for one thing; he put his ideas in words that would not occur to the average man. He had volunteered no information about himself. I didn't know how he had come to meet Mom in the orange grove, or why she felt he needed her help. If anyone were obviously capable of taking care of himself, that was Pat Thatcher. Perhaps the shoe was on the other foot. Maybe Thatcher attached himself to us because he knew we needed him.

Miles ahead of us, glittering like a fragment of glass lost in a pool of darkness, I could see Big Bear Lake, at the heart of a broad valley thickly grown with pines.

A highway turnout had been made at Lakeview Point. Hidden in the shadow we saw Willie Clapper's blue Cadillac, lying on its side precariously close to the edge. It had been overturned by the blast. Flying debris and soil particles had scoured off the paint on one side of the car.

Thatcher and I put down our cartons and moved toward the Cadillac cautiously. Thatcher pushed a shell into my rifle and carried it across his shoulder. We bellowed Clapper's name but got no reply. I climbed the frame and tried to pull open the door. It was locked and the car was empty.

Thatcher scratched his head with the barrel of the rifle.

"If Clapper's gone, he must have locked the car from the outside." There was a sudden sound in the trees above the turnout. Thatcher whirled, snapping the rifle to his shoulder. The noise wasn't repeated and warily he lowered the gun. It had been nothing.

Thatcher looked at the car again. "The way I figure it, Willie Clapper drove past us like a bat out of hell. Then he parked the car up here, got out and locked it up just before the bomb went off. It would have been suicide if he had been farther down the highway—no protection there at all. But if that's the way it stacks up, Clapper knew the bomb was going off—and he knew approximately when."

"How could he? That doesn't make sense. And where's Clapper now?"

"That's an interesting question, Jerry. Gone with the big wind—maybe. Your first one's easier; he was working with the Reds."

"Willie Clapper? Now I've heard everything."

We returned to the highway and picked up our cartons.

We made another quarter mile before Mom gave out. She dropped on the shoulder of the road, not quite unconscious but close to it. We improvised a camp close by in a small clearing sheltered by a V-shaped wall of rock.

Thatcher took the first watch. I knew I couldn't keep awake. My mind was in a daze, where nothing mattered very much. I had a nagging mistrust of Thatcher—an uneasy feeling...

When Pat Thatcher shook me awake I felt as if I hadn't slept at, all, yet I saw dawn in the eastern sky.

"We said we'd change off every few minutes, Pat!" It seemed entirely natural to use his first name. The suspicion I felt suddenly struck me as absurd.

"You looked as if you could use the rest, Jerry," Pat replied. "I found a spring about a hundred yards down the road. Go stick your head in it. The water's cold as hell, but it'll do you good."

At least it washed the cotton out of my head. When I walked back to the camp the chilly morning wind felt pleasantly cozy. Thatcher threw me the rifle and lay down on the pine bed beside Jim Riley. I crossed the road and sat on a boulder, watching the sunrise over the valley.

I thought of the people who had been trapped under the bomb. How many had died?—half a million; twice that?

I felt a hand on my shoulder. I turned. Cheryl Fineberg stood beside me, holding out her sweater.

"You looked so cold out here Jerry. Don't you want to put this on?"

I grinned and pushed my arms into the sleeves. Cheryl was a nice little thing to have around. It was the first time

I saw her simply as a girl.

Unfortunately Cheryl's sweater was too small. It pulled painfully against the abrasive burns on my back. I took it off again.

"Maybe I ought to start getting used to a few discomforts," I apologized.

"We all should, I guess." She folded the sweater carefully. "I'll put this aside. Your mother might really have to have it if—well, later on…"

Yes, later on: if we were still refugees in the mountains when winter came. So that possibility had occurred to Cheryl, too. She wasn't the kind of girl who tried to avoid an unpleasant fact by pretending it wasn't there.

"The morning is so beautiful, Jerry. It's hard to believe the nightmare last night was real."

"We were lucky. If we had gone on to the desert as we were supposed to—"

As I glanced in Cheryl's direction I saw, far up the road, a man walking toward us. I stood up, slipping my finger through the rifle guard. The sun rose over the ridge and in the slanting shaft of light on the highway I recognized Willie Clapper. He raised his hands high.

"Don't shoot!" he cried. "I'm a friend. I'm not armed." His voice was ragged with fear.

I motioned for him to join us. He ran forward eagerly. "My cabin was burned. I have no food. If you could spare me a little something to eat—" His wheedling trailed off hopefully.

"We met last night, Dr. Clapper," I said, "on the road. Perhaps you remember—"

"I was scared. I couldn't think straight."

"You deliberately started a second fire and tried to kill us."

"I thought you were— Well, the Reds would send subversives out to get me; I've fought the good fight so long."

From Willie Clapper's point of view, that nonsense was probably logical. "All right," I agreed. "You can eat with us."

Thatcher made no attempt to hide his anger when he saw Clapper; if the decision had been up to Pat, Clapper would have starved.

I thought Mom would be pleased to find herself so close to her idol. Instead, she was cold and aloof, remembering that Clapper had nearly run her down the night before.

I had made our fire at the back of the clearing. Sheltered by the rocks, we could not be seen from the road, nor were we able to see more than a twenty-foot segment of the highway. The Soviet paratrooper stumbled on us totally unprepared. We heard the indrawn breath from the mouth of the clearing.

For a second no one moved. We sat staring dumbly at the enemy; he stared back at us. His uniform was torn and smeared. His face seemed unusually red, as if he had stayed too long in the summer sun. He was carrying a submachine gun; he raised it slowly.

Willie Clapper sprang up. "Not me!" he yelped. "You know who I am. These others—"

Thatcher slammed his elbow into Clapper's stomach, and the politician dropped, groaning. Simultaneously Mom screamed and snatched my rifle, firing blindly.

The Soviet soldier toppled toward us. His gun clattered from his fingers. Cheryl caught it and bent over the man. "He's still alive," she said. "Your shot went wild, Mrs. Bonhill, I think he was hurt in the fire."

Cheryl looked at the submachine gun. She ran her fingers over the firing stud. "This may be the man who killed my father; he may be the man who dropped the bomb on the desert."

IX. The City—Friday morning, 2:30 A.M. Dr. Stewart Roswell

TWENTY-FOUR of us stood rigid against the cloister arches while General Anton Zergoff walked toward George Knight. Raw, heavy-muscled, animal power, a Goliath armed with whip and revolver and the absolute authority of the military conqueror—facing a slight, unimposing, beaten man, armed only with the intangible strength of conviction.

"The Quaker Pacifist," Zergoff purred. "The coward afraid to fight."

He lashed the back of his hand against Knight's jaw. The Quaker reeled, blood trickling from the freshly opened wounds in his lip. The General bent close to the smaller man's face.

"This is the idiot who betrayed Alexander Gordov. In a people's democracy, Comrade Knight, we are realists. I consider it my responsibility to educate you in the fundamental psychology of human nature." Zergoff swung his hand again; Knight staggered and I saw his eyes glaze with pain. "Every man will fight, Comrade Knight—every man, when it means his own survival. It shall be my pleasure to smash this bourgeois idealism of yours. And when you are broken, Comrade, you will work with us or face the firing squad—however the whim happens to strike me."

George Knight lifted his hand quietly. In a quiet, almost compassionate voice, he said, "And now, General, like your misguided friend—" He gestured toward Dragen "—now you will quote Christ's words and order me to turn the other cheek. The due of Caesar."

Zergoff stood for a moment clenching his fists. Then, slowly, he began to smile. "No, Comrade, I expect to apply a somewhat more realistic psychology."

He jerked a revolver from his belt, emptying it except for one shell. He put the weapon on the table, motioning the Soviet soldiers back against the wall. Watching Knight's face, he beckoned one of Dragen's bullyboys, disarmed the man and handed him a riding crop. He pushed Knight close to the table, where he stood two feet from the loaded revolver.

"A lesson, Comrade," Zergoff said, "in human nature. You should find the experiment illuminating. Comrade Bergoll, here, has always been obedient to party discipline. I am ordering him, under no condition, to touch the revolver. That weapon is for you to use; your only way to save yourself, incidentally. Comrade Bergoll will beat you with the crop until you break down and defend yourself. The gun's there, by your hand. Who knows? You might even reach it in time."

General Zergoff moved back with the Soviet soldiers. He gulped a stiff drink from the vodka bottle, then he signaled with a gesture, and the beating began. I felt a sick nausea. Somewhere among the prisoners I heard a man vomiting; Zergoff bellowed with laughter. "The party develops strong bellies," he said; "if you survive."

And all the while I heard the steady slash of the crop upon human flesh. Knight neither cried out nor resisted. The silence lengthened; it endured for an eternity.

Sudden fury distorted Zergoff's face and he ordered the torment to stop.

George Knight still stood beside the revolver, bleeding and almost unconscious. I thought he smiled; it was difficult to identify an expression in the pulp of his face.

"Is it possible, General," he asked, "that your psychology of human nature needs revision?"

"You won't destroy me the way you did Gordov!"

"General, before your experiment began, you admitted failure."

"I have not failed! On your knees you will confess—"

"If I believed in violence, when you left the gun on the table I would have used it against you, General. You knew I wouldn't. You knew you were safe."

General Zergoff hurled an unopened bottle at Knight. It struck Knight's head, and the Quaker collapsed on the floor. The bottle shattered against the wall. His face white, Zergoff moved toward Knight. With the toe of his boot he turned the Quaker on his back.

"Not dead," he grunted, with what seemed to me a tone of satisfaction. He snapped his fingers at his men. They propped Knight into a chair and tried to revive him.

Zergoff faced us, pacing up and down while he talked; slowly he regained confidence.

"You have seen a demonstration of our methods of education. The lesson should be clear to you all."

Was he so accustomed to success, to the Communist formula of fear that he didn't know what he was saying? The lesson was there: we had watched the conqueror admit defeat. Knight had given each of us the will to resist in our own way, armed with our individual beliefs. Anton Zergoff had missed the point.

"We have a use for each of you," the General went on. "You can serve us painlessly or after indoctrination. The choice is yours.

"Los Angeles is our key to victory. Beginning at dawn we shall funnel manpower into this area—according to the present plan, approximately five thousand men an hour. We have transformed the war into an infantry conflict; with all of Europe, Asia and Africa to draw from, we hold the overwhelming superiority in manpower. On both sides the atomic weapon is finished. Production capacity has been destroyed. Your air force as well as ours has been reduced to a negligible factor. True, your navy is still intact. But we have submarines in the Los Angeles harbor to hold off any direct naval attack.

"I am telling you this—the full, strategic picture—so you will understand that our victory is inevitable. We ask your help in order to bring the day of peace closer and spare your people the futile sacrifice of a long infantry war.

"We will go on the air at noon, on a twenty-four hour basis. We expect each of you to speak for us to your fellow citizens. Nothing really different from what you have already said or written, nothing different from what you believe yourselves. Can you honestly call that propaganda? Can you still say we are not sincerely humanitarian, not—"

An officer came to the door. Zergoff turned toward him. "Well?" he snapped.

"He has left the city, Comrade General."

"The fool! The heart of a rabbit. Have you traced him?"

"It is probable that he went to some sort of a vacation house—"

"Find it."

The officer saluted and turned away. As Zergoff swung toward us again, he saw that George Knight had regained consciousness. The General took the revolver from the table and ambled toward Knight's chair, smiling with smug self-confidence.

"Possibly, Comrade Knight, my original approach to your re-education was wrong. Here is the weapon I gave you before, still loaded with the one shell you refused to use to defend yourself. Take it, Comrade."

Knight did not move. Zergoff shrugged and balanced the revolver on the arm of the Quaker's chair. "You would not fight for yourself —but of course you would defend a helpless man. Typical middle-class nobility. Surely, Comrade, you would sacrifice your soul to save another man?"

"If it were the will of God."

Zergoff selected a prisoner at random. He ordered Bergoll to lash this new victim with the riding crop.

"Take the gun, Comrade. If you fire at Bergoll, the beating will stop."

Knight held his hands folded in his lap. The prisoner cried out in agony; blood spilled from his lacerated face. In Knight's eyes I saw a surge of pity, as if he felt the pain himself.

"Here is an innocent man." Zergoff bent toward the Quaker, no longer smiling and no longer confident. "A persecuted man. You can save him—at the sacrifice of a principle. You lose nothing real. No property; no money. It costs you nothing, Pacifist!"

"Nor would I save him."

Zergoff clenched his fists. Slowly the color drained from his face. "Comrade if you will fire the gun —simply fire it, Comrade!—I will give you your freedom. You can leave this house and go where you please. You have my promise as a Soviet General."

"And all I hear is the voice of a Soviet General—not the

inner voice of God."

The prisoner fell and Zergoff, quivering with anger, waved Bergoll aside. He snapped one of his men to attention and took his submachine gun. Grinning again he carried the gun to Knight and laid it gently in his lap.

"Now, Comrade, fire," he whispered. "You can kill us all; you can destroy the high command of the invasion."

George Knight did not touch the gun. He glanced up at Zergoff and he said gently, "You know this experiment is safe, too, General. I will not use the gun."

Zergoff leaped at him, hammering Knight's face with his fists. When the General's fury subsided, the Quaker was unconscious again. Zergoff said drunkenly, "Send them back to their rooms. Dragen, get me a bottle."

I carried George Knight up the three flights of carpeted steps. As I lowered him into the chair, his eyes fluttered open. In a whisper he said, "Thank God I—I had the strength to go through with it."

He lapsed into unconsciousness. I stood looking at him, and I knew I saw a miracle.

Part Two

The First Two Days

I. *The Highway—Friday, 9:00 A.M. Boris Yorovich*

I SAW the redheaded girl first, looking down at me. Her face was hard, but the expression was something new to her. It didn't fit her well. Behind the grimness I saw a sensitive, clear-eyed innocence, like the farm girls on our party posters. She had my submachine gun in her hand; it was aimed steadily at my heart.

"You're going to kill me?" I asked.

"Not yet."

Americans were softhearted fools, the commissars had always told us. The tension in my muscles relaxed. If I rolled against her legs, I could knock her down and take the gun from her. I tentatively tried to move my legs and I felt the numb pain again. I wasn't sure I could walk. That damned fire! …

"I'm surprised you speak English," the girl said. "That will make it easier—what we have to do."

"We were ordered to learn your language for the invasion."

I turned my head and I saw the others. An elderly couple, a dark-haired man with a politician's slick face, a child, and a boy about the girl's age—a big, half-naked, giant, who looked like a Finn or a Swede. He might be the redhead's husband, but I didn't think they married so early in America.

"You have a name," the girl said.

"Boris Yorovich, Lieutenant, Soviet Paratroops." That much we were permitted to tell them.

"I'm Cheryl Fineberg." She told me the names of the others, and I was baffled. I thought this was a family unit—the Americans cling together with typical middle-class loyalty, the commissars had said —but only the blond giant and the old woman had the same family name.

The girl tossed my gun to the old man and bent over me, ripping the torn uniform away from my leg. The hot pain was like fire when she touched my skin.

"It's a nasty cut," she said, "and you're badly burned." She opened a small, canvas bag and stood tiny bottles and tubes of medicine on the ground until she found the drug she wanted. "This should kill the infection, Lieutenant Yorovich. Afterward, we'll put a salve on those burns. How did you get hurt?"

"Our transport was shot down. We tried to use our chutes, but we were caught on the wing. I was lucky. Just before the crash, I got free. A tree broke my fall. It scratched me up a little, but that's all."

"And the others?" She sprinkled a sulfa powder over, my wound.

I was tempted to lie to her—perhaps that's our natural approach to every situation—but it might have made her less willing to help me. "The fuel tank caught fire," I explained. "They were burned to death. It was a close call for me, too. Before I got out of that tree, the forest around me was burning. It was hot as hell."

"It was hot, I'm sure, Lieutenant," she agreed, "but not as hot as the H-bombs you dropped on our cities." Her innocence, then, had teeth to it. Maybe this wouldn't be the pushover I expected.

Why had they kept me alive? Why had she tended my wounds? We were enemies. The Americans must have hated us. I felt no hatred for them, of course; pity, perhaps, that a system so attractive had to be destroyed because it was too weak to defend itself.

I count myself a sophisticate—or, rather, I did then. I was nineteen; I had been a university student for more than a year. I knew the difference between truth and party double-talk, but I also knew what I had to do to survive.

The girl motioned to the half-naked blond, whose name was Jerry Bonhill. He put his hands beneath my shoulders and lifted me to my feet. I staggered back against the rocky wall rising above the clearing.

Each of the others spoke to me, except the handsome politician, Dr. Willard Clapper. He mentioned his Cadillac. It was an issue they had been talking about before I stumbled into the clearing. I leaned against the granite, listening. I gathered that the politician's automobile had overturned. He wanted their help to right it so he could escape. No mention of them; just his own, personal survival. A good party man: yes, that man I understood.

Still it didn't add up right. This Clapper was the type who knew the angles and the risks. He must have known he was safer right here than anywhere else. The leather-faced old man — Pat Thatcher—put an end to the talk by saying flatly,

"We have another use for your car, Clapper."

"It is my duty as an American —a loyal American, I may add—to offer my services to the government."

"We'll be better off at Big Bear; so we'll use your car to get there."

"Time is of the essence, Thatcher! Under the best of conditions it's a three-hour drive to Los Angeles—"

"And just what do you have to do there?"

"I used that—I used it only as a comparative distance."

The politician's voice shot up into the high registers as the old man clutched his coat and lifted him two inches off the ground.

"Let me have the key, Clapper."

Dr. Clapper fumbled in his coat pocket and handed over a key ring. I began to envy the way they handled their politicians in America. Maybe if we had done the same thing long ago, we could have called our souls our own now.

Thatcher and Jerry Bonhill went up the road toward the ridge. Clapper followed after them, bleating about loyalty and property rights. When they were gone, Bonhill's mother brought me some food in partly empty tins. Cheryl Fineberg stood thirty feet away, holding my machine gun and looking for all the world like a partisan guerilla on a party war poster.

I emptied the tins. Jim Riley, the child, asked me if I wanted something else. I said I did. He rummaged through the cartons of food, reading off the labels to me.

"Spaghetti and meatballs." I stopped him there. "That sounds fine, kid."

I took a meatball out of the can and offered it to the boy. He stuffed it into his cheek, like a squirrel with a nut.

"You know, you aren't such a bad guy," he decided.

The Cadillac came down the highway; it was painted blue on one side, while the bare metal was exposed on the other. Pat Thatcher was driving. Bonhill and Clapper sat beside him, and the politician was still whining about his rights.

"Of course it's my fault," Clapper admitted. "I didn't stop to fill the tank on my way up here. But that isn't the question. If we drive to Big Bear, I won't have enough gas left to—"

"It looks as if you aren't going anywhere, Dr. Clapper," Jerry said mildly.

"You have no legal right to interfere. This car is mine!"

"And we're using it."

These Americans were inexplicable. Without hesitation, they were applying something very close to Communism in seizing the politician's Cadillac. Maybe the Politburo psychologists were all wrong. Maybe the Americans valued the human being even above personal possessions. If so, that was a major error in our calculations. In a sense, it gave them a secret weapon that could win the war—if they knew how to exploit it properly.

We packed the canned goods in the trunk of the car. After a brief hesitation, Cheryl Fineberg shoved the submachine gun as well as Bonhill's rifle into the compartment and slammed down the lid. The two women, the boy and I sat in back. Thatcher was forced to drive very slowly along the winding road.

Jim Riley piped up, "We can't let them see the Lieutenant, not in his uniform. I don't think they'd understand that he's O.K."

"So you've made up your mind about him?" the girl asked.

"Yes," I laughed, "because I eat spaghetti for breakfast."

"Maybe that isn't such a bad standard of judgment, until we come up with something better," she answered seriously. "But Jim is right. Let's get rid of your coat, Lieutenant. And your rank along with it. From now on in you're simply Boris Yorovich, a friend we picked up on the road."

I slid off my coat, inching the scorched cloth over my blistered hands. She decided my woolen undershirt had to go, too. The military dye and the shoddy workmanship were a dead giveaway. Stripped naked to the waist; I made a poor contrast to the blond giant in the front seat. The redhead eyed me abstractly.

"We'll have to get you out in the sun, Boris. If you're typical, maybe what you Russians really need is a good, two-week vacation in the mountains—instead of another piece of someone else's territory."

With all our endless manpower, with all our planes and bombs, we had one small chance of victory—and only one. I saw that with a terrible clarity. If Willard Clapper were the average American, they would surrender in a week. But if Cheryl Fineberg and Jim Riley and Jerry Bonhill were the enemy—

Cheryl decided that my trousers, charred, dirty and torn, would be unidentifiable, but my boots had to go. She rolled the discards into a bundle and threw them from the open window. Dr. Clapper glanced at me across the front seat; his eyes glowed furiously.

"You know what you've done, Lieutenant Yorovich," he said. "The deliberate removal of a uniform is desertion. On the other hand, if you fall into the hands of responsible Americans—loyal Americans—you will be considered a spy. It isn't a happy situation, is it? As a human being, I wish I could help you."

As Clapper turned his head toward the front again, Mrs. Bonhill gave a little scream. "Stop, Mr. Thatcher! There's a man lying in the road."

Thatcher jammed on the brakes. The man moved, pushing himself up on his elbows. His face and arms were burned. The skin hung loose in flapping, tattered tendrils.

"A refugee from the desert," Jerry said.

"Burned by radiation!" Cheryl gasped. "We'll have to help him. Perhaps in the village we can find some drugs to—"

"You won't put him in my car!" Clapper yelped. "He

might be radioactive."

With a gesture of disgust, Thatcher opened the door and got out. Jerry Bonhill and Cheryl followed him.

Clapper moved to release the brake, so the car would roll down on the man and solve the problem for him. I reached across the seat and cracked my fist into the politician's jaw—three times, before the body went limp.

I felt exultant, as if I were mildly intoxicated. The feeling was very pleasant.

I got out and limped toward the others, to help them carry the groaning Negro to the car.

In that moment my choice was made. Not Clapper, but Cheryl and Bonhill were the spirit of America—the America we would never destroy. I could no longer bury inside my mind the whisper from my childhood; I no longer had a desire to do so.

II. The City—Friday Dr. Stewart Roswell

IN SPITE of General Zergoff's determination to put what he called our intellectual circus on the air at noon, the broadcast was postponed. Zergoff had a logical rationalization, as the Soviet Man must; the confusion in the United States on the first day of conquest was too widespread for the propaganda to be effective. His real reason was something a Russian General doesn't report to the Politburo: the spiritual challenge of George Knight, Quaker.

Twice during the night guards carried Knight out of our third-floor prison for long sessions of Communist re-education. When they brought him back the second time, shortly after dawn on Friday, the Quaker was close to death. Zergoff sent doctors to patch up the wounds. It wouldn't do for Knight to die—not until he admitted defeat.

Later Knight and I were both transferred to the first floor. We were still prisoners, but now we had the silk glove treatment in place of the mailed fist. George Knight, carefully bandaged and reeking of antiseptic, was laid on a leather couch and wrapped in blankets. Maria D'Orlez brought us a splendid breakfast—the only meal, incidentally, which we had that day.

Knight was still unconscious, but started to wake up after she left.

"During my educational indoctrination," Knight said when he had eaten a bit, "I did a great deal of meditating, Stewart. The world has been thrown into a disastrous war; the destruction is beyond any horror we can imagine; and the worst misery and torment for the homeless millions is still to come. Yet, in spite of all that, we have an opportunity to create something good out of this catastrophe. There will be no victor; there never is in war. But there can be an enormous victory of ideals—to put it in words that mean more to me: a spiritual victory. The fighting will one day end; it must. And a shattered world will have to be remade. Before we dream of cities and parks rising over the bomb craters, we must think—this time —about man himself. We must build a believing world. Belief is a fundamental need of us all."

"Belief in what, Knight? Belief is an abstract. Civilizations before ours have gone berserk in the name of belief."

"Let's say, to start with, belief in man—in the dignity of the human soul. Build on that—it's what I mean by a believing world—and the isms lose all significance."

He had made his point so unexpectedly it exploded in

my mind like a physical blow. "This mutual respect of each man for the other," I said. "By its very nature, it would wipe out Communism."

Knight shrugged his shoulders slightly. "Then, I'm afraid Zergoff believes in a false god. I'm truly sorry for him, Stewart. I say that in complete sincerity. It isn't easy for any man to have the fundamental nature of his being torn apart—even when it's built upon falsehood."

"And they call you Quakers Pacifists!"

"We take arms against no man, Stewart. But we believe all men—including ourselves—have the right to seek the inner voice of God in their own individual ways. I will die for that belief just as readily as Zergoff would die on the battlefield. The General can't recognize the conflict on my terms, precisely as I refuse to fight on his."

"But you're forcing him to fight on yours."

"Not at all. He's forcing himself."

"A man can't be a conscientious objector in a psychological war."

"Spiritual, please; why are educated people, so unwilling to use that word? And you're wrong, Stewart. General Zergoff can refuse to fight—I do wish you wouldn't call it that!—by having me executed whenever it pleases him."

"By doing that now—after he's told the rest of us he'll break you —it would be admitting defeat. Either way you win."

"It isn't a question of winning. It's the mutual respect we must learn to have for each other as human beings."

While Knight and I were talking, we could hear voices in the adjoining room, which General Zergoff was using as a staff office. Suddenly the pitch went higher and we were able to make out the words clearly.

"You've had ten hours, and all you produce is excuses."

Zergoff paused and when he spoke again each word was spaced like the boom of a cannon. "I want Willard Clapper here by noon. Check the refugee detail. If Clapper's trying to get back here, he'll be somewhere on the road.

"Then send a car up for him. He'd wait in the mountains for us to pick him up—I agree with you there. He'd know he couldn't get through to headquarters today without our help."

The voices simmered down.

Knight said, "Apparently, Stewart, you were right about Dr. Clapper. That appears to be obvious."

"If they put Clapper on the air with us—"

"The accuser and his victims, all joining hands in the noble cause of Soviet brotherhood." The Quaker chuckled. "It has amusing possibilities, as a radio show. I'm afraid it won't come off. Our intellectuals seem somewhat unwilling to co-operate."

"Largely as a result of your example."

"You give me too much credit. Perhaps I helped each of you see more clearly your own spiritual convictions; that's all."

Late in the afternoon the General found time for an interview with me. I thought I had been brought downstairs with Knight as a matter of convenience. But I discovered that Zergoff had specific plans for me. I was to be a sort of intellectual Judas, with my own neck at stake.

Zergoff came straight to the point. They had made recordings of my conversations with Knight, and the General believed the Quaker put unusual value upon my opinion. I was, therefore, ordered to persuade Knight to meet Zergoff's terms.

"You think I can do what you haven't?" I asked. "Suppose I refuse?"

"You will be shot." His voice was calm and self-assured. Fear prickled at the roots of my hair; I knew he meant precisely what he said. He added, "If I liquidate you, Dr. Roswell, I lose only one man. Granted, you have some use to us, but you are expendable. You have taken no romantic moral stand in front of the others."

"But George Knight has."

"Exactly. He is setting the pace for the rest of you."

The door of the nook slid open. Zergoff looked up at a saluting subordinate. "Sir, the report on Clapper—"

"You've found him?"

"We sent a jeep into the mountains. Three men, commanded by a sergeant; all we could spare at the time. We have had no communication from them in six hours; we presume they're lost to guerilla action."

"American guerillas? Don't be a fool; these bourgeoisie wouldn't have the backbone—" Zergoff got a grip on his

anger. "Send another truck—this time with enough men to do the job."

The junior officer saluted and departed. Zergoff strode toward the door. He glanced at me and, more or less as an afterthought, he added, "One other point you should understand, Dr. Roswell: I'm giving you a deadline—eight o'clock tonight..."

My only problem was how much I should tell Knight. Although our spoken conversation was monitored, I could have written the facts and passed them over to him while we chatted of inconsequential things. For some fifteen minutes I sat facing him, talking bland nonsense, while I tried to make up my mind. And then even that problem no longer mattered.

We heard the sound of far away explosions in the harbor and a sudden scurrying of booted feet out of the living room.

The explosions were suddenly closer. A plane screamed overhead. The wall burst open, in a blinding chaos of smoke and flying debris. I was flung against the couch. Books rained down on Knight and me, shielding us from the glass that flew out of the narrow windows.

Dazed, I pulled myself to my feet. I saw that the sidewall was gone, open to the alley back of the house. It meant escape. At least a slim chance. Better than staying where we were. I lifted Knight in my arms and stumbled toward the opening.

Fire was licking at the house as I carried George Knight through the torn wall. The alley outside seemed to be clear. But suddenly a Communist soldier—an enormous man—loomed out of the shadows.

"Are you Americans?" he asked.

I swung my fist; he caught it in his huge hand.

"My name is Chen Phiang," he whispered close to my ear. "I am Chinese. I want to help you. Come, I will show you a place to hide."

After a moment, I followed him toward the side street. Flak from anti-aircraft shells was falling everywhere. Close by on the boulevard fire blazed against the dusk sky. I saw the broken skeleton of a fallen plane. The Chinese took George Knight in his arms.

"I am Chen Phiang," he said again. "I have at last remembered the wisdom of my paternal grandparent."

III. The City—Friday at dusk Chen Phiang

I AM ONLY seventeen. I have a poor memory of my paternal grandparent, who was a tea merchant in Hong Kong. He came frequently to visit my father's shop in Canton. I listened carefully when he spoke, because in those days we honored the wisdom of our elders.

The soldiers of the people's government took me from

my father's shop when I was very small. I remember my mother's tears and my father's terror. My mother held me against her heart. A soldier struck her with his rifle.

My father was a landowner and an enemy of the people. They told me that much later, at a school in Pekin, and I believed them, because they were skillful teachers. It was right for my mother and my father to be liquidated; I believed that, too, for I was a conscientious student. The teachers said I would not be a good citizen until I wiped away every memory of my parents and my grandparents.

At fifteen I began my military training. Six months later, because I was large and strong and quick thinking, I was transferred to the paratroops. Our training was rigid. When we were not practicing in the planes our Russian allies gave us, we were hardening our muscles with athletic drills and hand-to-hand conflict. One hour each morning we had classes for political indoctrination; four hours every night we learned English.

During the indoctrination sessions, special political officers came from Pekin to explain current news. We had one mortal enemy, they told us: the Fascist government of the United States, which kept its own people in ignorance and slavery.

I know, now, it was all a lie. My heart is burning with the taste of betrayal. I was a part of it. I marched blindly with the others.

I learned to hate the enemy with a terrible loathing, for I had cousins who lived in the United States. We had never met; it surprised me that they were even aware of my humble existence. Yet, from time to time, the political officer from Pekin brought me letters from my cousins— pitiful, tragic pleas for us to release them from their reactionary masters. Many of the men in my corps had similar letters from their own kin. Our hatred was inflamed.

On the day our Russian allies were forced to occupy Paris to protect the people from the Wall Street plutocrats, our military corps was ordered to leave Pekin.

Our corps flew north to a Russian base in Siberia, a new field more elaborately camouflaged than anything I had ever seen.

The paratroopers packed into the dugouts were all approximately my age; they had all been separated from their parents in early childhood and reared in government schools.

During the two days of our confinement the only language we were permitted to speak was English. The officers gave us American newspapers and periodicals to read.

Toward the end of the second day we heard the bombers overhead. The commissar ordered us out of our hammocks. We crowded together in front of the television screen. Automatic transmitters set up in the cities showed us the holocaust of the bombing, until the transmitters themselves were destroyed. Moscow, Pekin, Shanghai, Canton, Bombay, Leningrad, Berlin, Madrid: we watched them die. Our homes, the cities we prided, the people we knew as friends—destroyed by the sneak attack of American planes. Undeclared war.

The commissar brought us liquor. We smashed the empty bottles against the earthen wall, as we would have smashed the enemy.

Shortly before dawn—I am not sure of the hour, because I had drunk myself into a stupor—we were loaded into the transports.

I slept until a needle pricked my arm. I opened my eyes

and saw the commissar jerk out the empty hypodermic. "You'll feel fine in a minute," he said as he moved on to the next man.

Half an hour later we made the jump. Ours was not the first wave of the invasion. Soviet paratroops had landed during the night and seized key points. The morning sun was bright and clear as I parachuted toward Los Angeles.

I checked in at the nearest Soviet guard post. The Lieutenant in charge recorded my identification number and assigned me to the refugee detail. Our job was to un-snarl the traffic and get the people off the streets.

An interminable flood of cars continued to crowd in from the desert. And this, I thought, was happening on all the highways leading into the city. By weight of numbers alone the Americans could have subdued us. They seemed unaware of that.

By mid-afternoon my drugged god-feeling was gone. I had to hold to my post doggedly, fighting fatigue. My nerves were raw. I screamed orders at the prisoners, sometimes forgetting to speak in English. I used my gun more frequently, on very little provocation. My only emotion was hatred.

A very old, very crowded automobile came toward us. The motor was coughing; steam shot from the open radiator. I strode toward it, swinging my submachine gun angrily.

The motor stalled again. A rear door banged open and four children spilled out; the eldest was no more than nine. They began to plead with me in their shrill, childish voices. Please, would I be patient? Their mother was sick; she had been burned by the bomb.

Their words made no impression, but their faces did.

For they were Chinese. Chinese like myself.

The man got out. He began to address me awkwardly in Cantonese.

"I speak English," I told him proudly.

His face relaxed. "Sir, my wife is very ill. A doctor examined her; he said she might possibly live if—"

"What are you doing with these Fascist pigs?"

He looked me straight in the eye. "I am an American." He said it without shame. With a dignity that made me writhe, he returned to the car and lifted out his wife. A white man from another vehicle came and talked to him. They put the Chinese woman in the second car; a white woman slid behind the wheel, after first making a pillow of her coat and sliding it behind the Chinese woman's head.

That unexpected gesture of kindness gave me my first doubt. The letters from my cousin had said that the Chinese, without exception, were the most persecuted slaves of capitalism. Yet now, with my own eyes, I had seen a white family help a Chinese woman.

The four children climbed into the second car. Since there was no one left to drive the wreck belonging to the Chinese, I ordered four prisoners to push it into a side street, to clear the road. Until it was out of the way, the second car was stalled, and all the long column of vehicles behind it. The eldest Chinese child—a girl—got out and walked toward me.

"Do you know a working class man whose name is Lin Yeng?" I asked her.

"You talk in such a foolish way. What's a working class? The only kind of classes I know about are the ones in school, and we don't work unless we have to."

My nerves began to tense in anger again; the tone of my voice went up a notch. "Do you know Lin Yeng?" I repeated.

"No, but lots of Chinese live in Los Angeles.

"How would I find Lin Yeng?" I asked. "He's a cousin of mine; we have corresponded for many years."

"Try the phone book. But take a tip from me, soldier; I don't think he's going to give you the red carpet treatment."

Late in the afternoon we were relieved at the barricade by fresh troops. I reported back to the guard post. The Lieutenant gave me my billet assignment in a hotel overlooking the public bathing beach, a mile or so south of the harbor.

I ate in the hotel dining room, at a table with two infantry privates and a Russian air force sergeant. It was a magnificent meal. We had all the food and liquor of a captured city at our disposal.

During a lull I asked—simply to be saying something, not because it really mattered to me—I asked why we were so sure the American counterattack would come from the sea.

The sergeant spoke up, "I was in one of the planes. I saw the orders. We built a wall around the city, so we could have time to bring our troops in." He drank and the whiskey spilled down his chin. "Not a real wall, you understand. But it works the same. We dropped a ring of baby H-bombs all around the city, a couple of hundred miles back from the coast. One hell of a big ditch. And it'll stay radioactive maybe a week. After that they can cross it—if they wear the right equipment—but by that time it'll be too late."

So the bombs had been ours. We had murdered defenseless people.

I gulped the rest of my meal. It was tasteless. I left the

dining room. The hotel lobby was jammed with our troops, all very drunk.

I saw a telephone booth and I remembered what the Chinese girl had said. In the directory I read through the listings until I found the name of Lin Yeng. I copied the address on a scrap of paper.

His address was south of the hotel, two city blocks back from the beachfront boulevard.

The houses behind the boulevard were less imposing, although still larger than anything I was accustomed to. Lin Yeng's address was in a small, secondary shopping district. I passed a vast hall, called a super-market, a drug store, and a cleaning establishment, before I saw Lin Yeng's place of business —a Chinese restaurant on the corner. His name in large gold letters was painted on the window.

I walked down a narrow alley. Dangerous, perhaps, in an enemy city, but I was well armed. Behind some of the shops there were living quarters. Lin Yeng had an apartment over a big garage, where I saw a gleaming car called a Cadillac as well as a delivery truck with my cousin's name painted on the panel. My cousin? No, this must be another Lin Yeng. My cousin was a worker. He had told me that many times in his letters. It had to be true; still, something within me drove me to make certain.

In the apartment I saw a light. I crept up the outer steps, until I could see through a partly opened window, where the curtain had been drawn not quite to the sill. The room was furnished with all the magnificence of a party official's residence: many comfortable chairs, a lounge, Chinese scrolls on the wall, jade work standing on a side table, at least four reading lamps—in one room!—a tremendous radio, and a television set. This Lin Yeng must have been a very rich plutocrat to be able to afford a private television screen for his own family alone.

In an adjoining room I saw two pretty Chinese girls—both my age, or a little younger—at a dining table. A man and a woman, beyond my restricted line of vision, were talking.

"This cousin of yours in China, my dear—do you suppose he's still safe?"

"Chen Phiang?" the man asked in a distressed voice. "No, they would dispose of him now."

"But you sent all that money so faithfully for so many years!"

"Blackmail. Chen Phiang is no use to them anymore. We did all we could to help him; we must remember that. Maybe they were kind enough to give him a merciful death."

I stole away, dazed and sick at heart from what I had heard. This was my cousin; I could no longer doubt that. He had paid party blood money in order to help me, a stranger he had never met. To help me!—and now I stood at his door in the uniform of the conqueror. I felt the anguish of shame and dishonor.

I reached the oceanfront close to the palace. Two Russian sentries, armed with automatic rifles, challenged me. I fumbled blindly for words. One of them jerked open my tunic and looked at my identification disc. Their military manner relaxed.

"Out on the prowl, soldier?"

"Everything was—locked up," I stammered. I motioned toward the men in front of the big house. "What's all this for?"

"Command headquarters. General Zergoff." The sentry said.

"There's another reason for the guard," the second sentry put in, to make sure I'd be properly impressed. "We have twenty-five prisoners inside. American intellectuals. After the Comrade General finishes their re-education, they'll sing their song to our tune."

"I thought all intellectuals were enemies of the people."

"They're for the firing squad; you can be sure of that." The Russian grinned. "After we're through with them."

We heard a roar of planes. Every eye turned toward the sky. Anti-aircraft guns in the harbor began to spit angrily. One of the sentries cried, "A Fascist raid!" They began to run for cover.

I stood where I was, paralyzed with inner horror and disgust, the last bitter ash of shame.

Then a phosphorous shell from an attacking plane burst over the harbor and in the white glare I saw the rows upon rows of Soviet submarines.

Since the Soviet submarines were already in the American port, they must have left their Asiatic pens more than a week ago, under orders to begin the invasion. That had been at least four days before the crisis began.

Built upon that fact, everything else formed a single, terrifying pattern: the English they made us learn; our practice jumps over a plain marked with the streets of Los Angeles; the new, elaborately camouflaged Siberian bases, where the invasion troops had been safely concealed from American bombers. Protesting humanitarianism, screaming peace and brotherhood, we had planned this war for years.

Somewhere a soldier shouted at me, "Take cover, fool!"

I was behind the headquarters mansion, in a narrow alley. The guards were gone. I was alone.

Suddenly a plane soared directly overhead, out of control. A bomb exploded under the bluff and the earth rocked. Another hit the headquarters palace. Debris and dust and flying plaster flew in my face, flinging me back against a wall. I saw a tongue of fire licking at the gapping hole torn in the side of the house. The plane crashed in the street; the fuel tank caught fire.

In the orange glare I saw two men stumble through the broken wall. One was so badly wounded his face was unrecognizable; the second man was carrying him. They were not in uniform. They must, then, be two of the intellectuals imprisoned in the house.

I leaped toward them. They shrank away, trying to run. I caught the arm of the man who was unhurt. "Are you Americans?" I demanded.

Instead of replying, the man swung his fist at me weakly.

"My name is Chen Phiang," I said. "I am Chinese; I want to help you. Come, I will show you a place to hide."

My shame and dishonor diminished a little. This my paternal grandparent approved; one small thing to make amends for the red nightmare that had so long swallowed up the soul of China.

IV. The Valley—Friday afternoon Boris Yorovich

TWENTY minutes after we picked up the wounded Negro, Pat Thatcher pulled the Cadillac to a stop in the village of Big Bear. It was the first American town I had ever seen.

We stopped in front of a drug store. Pat Thatcher got out and pounded on the door, while Jerry Bonhill and I lifted the Negro out of the car.

Having raised no one by his knocking, Thatcher wrapped the tail of his shirt around his fist and smashed open the window in the door. He slipped his hand through the glass and turned the lock. Bonhill and I carried the Negro into the building. The old man shoved a display of stuffed toys from a table and we lay the Negro on it.

Cheryl Fineberg and Mrs. Bonhill came in with Jim Riley. Dr. Clapper remained outside on the step, watching us but refusing to have any part in our invasion of private property. The women cut away the clothing from the Negro's arms, while Thatcher brought jars of salve from a side shelf.

"People," the Negro whispered in a choked voice barely audible. "I found people?"

"You'll be all right now."

"There are others. Help..." His voice trailed off. Mrs. Bonhill stooped beside him and slipped her arm under his head. After a moment he spoke again, his thick, torn lips close to her ear. "They're back on the hill. On the hill. All right except—except tired. Please help them. They need..."

His head slumped forward. Mrs. Bonhill bent over his chest. Then she stood up slowly, her eyes filmed with tears. "He's dead."

"Put up your hands." A voice sounded behind us.

We swung around to face a small, plump, white-haired woman wearing a gingham dress and ankle-high mountain boots, gray with dust. She held a hunting rifle aimed at us unwaveringly.

"Sorry, ma'am," Thatcher apologized. "We didn't know anyone was here." He gestured toward the Negro. "We were trying to get drugs for—"

"You're from the city?"

"We'll pay for what we've used."

"This isn't my store. You're welcome to it."

The plump woman seemed less suspicious. She shot a glance suddenly at Cheryl, demanding her name and her

street address. The woman asked Mrs. Bonhill the same question. The two answers seemed to satisfy her. She nodded and muttered, "That fits." Abruptly she lowered her gun. "I had to make sure you weren't Reds."

"These people are subversives," Clapper hissed from the door. He pointed at me. "That man's a Russian officer. They stole my car. If you'll make Thatcher give me my keys—"

"Dr. Clapper was the only one of you I recognized. If he says you're subversives, that makes you fine in my book."

Clapper turned and stormed off down the street. The woman laughed. "He won't go far." She told us her name was Virginia Grant. She was a retired high school history teacher.

"You're the only one who stayed?"

"No, Henry Jenkins is here, too. Hank, we call him. An old loafer who has an idea he's going to strike gold over in Holcomb Valley. As soon as it dawned on him this morning that we were alone, he started out to drink up all the liquor in Big Bear. He's still in one of the saloons, I imagine."

"The Negro told us there were survivors somewhere in the hills," Cheryl Fineberg put in. "We'll have to try to find them."

"We might pick up his trail and back-track on it," Jerry Bonhill suggested.

"You men do that," the teacher decided. "While you're gone, we'll work out some sort of housing arrangement."

"I wish we could get some news," she continued. "Ben Canster had all sorts of fancy equipment in his appliance shop, but I can't seem to get it hitched up right. Ben didn't use regular electric outlets. He has his own Delco plant, and I don't know how to make the thing go."

I volunteered, "Maybe I could help, Miss Grant. We had a good deal of basic electronics in our training for—" I caught the slip. "That is, in the school I was attending."

"Stay here and see what you can do," Thatcher suggested. "Jerry and I can round up the survivors."

Before they left, Thatcher drove the Negro's body to a pine-sheltered knoll overlooking the lake, where Virginia Grant said we could bury him. While I scooped a shallow grave in the soft earth, she sent Jim Riley to carry stones up from the lakeside and pile them into a pyramided marker. With a teacher's eye for detail, she made two legible copies of the Negro's name and address from the driver's license she found in his wallet.

"We must keep an accurate record," she said. "Someday his family may want to locate the body."

Cheryl Fineberg and I were alone by the grave. Cheryl helped me tramp the soil over the body.

Virginia Grant rejoined us then. We finished the Negro's grave and walked back to the village. The teacher took us to Ben Canster's appliance shop, where she had earlier broken open the display room door. In a back room I found an elaborate, all-frequency-receiving apparatus. It was easy to put it in operation. The receiver was powered by a Delco electric unit, driven by a gas motor, which made the receiver independent of the regular electric supply.

Jim Riley and I explored the back of the appliance shop. In a separate, frame building we found a radio transmitter. Ben Canster spared nothing for his hobby. It was a magnificent transmitter in excellent order, and powered like the receiver by the independent Delco unit. While I was testing it, we heard uncertain footsteps on the gravel outside. A tall, thin, old man, his white hair uncombed and a gray stubble on his chin, staggered to the door. He was wearing khaki trousers, a frayed, cotton shirt, and very battered boots; he stank of sweat and liquor.

"That you, Ben?" he asked, peering into the semi-darkness.

"It must be Hank Jenkins," Jim Riley whispered to me.

I held out my hand. "My name's Yorovich."

"Russian! You guys got here damn fast. Might know you'd smell out all this liquor."

The boy said, "No, we're refugees from Los Angeles—"

"All the worse. City people! Always drink up everything in sight. No moderation. Well, I got the Double Seven staked out; you ain't gettin' in there."

He stumbled away, weaving down the street and humming an off-key melody.

It was after one o'clock that afternoon when Jim Riley came running over from the hotel to tell us Bonhill and Thatcher were back. "And we're going to have dinner right away."

"Did they find the survivors?"

"Sure. Two ladies and a colored boy." Jim's eyes sparkled. "His name is Ted Fisher and he's just my age and he wasn't hurt at all!"

The two women Bonhill and Thatcher had rescued were both in their thirties.

The taller of the two, a slim blonde, whose name was Janice Gage, was very attractive—except for the shadow of horror in her gray eyes. The other refugee, small, brown-haired, pert-faced, was Lola Donne, a buxom, sensuous woman who seemed on the verge of overflowing the tight dress she wore.

While we ate, they told us what had happened on the desert. The two women were strangers. Each of them, in separate cars, had been among the first evacuees to leave Los Angeles.

Near Lucerne Valley they were caught in the frantic exodus of automobiles coming down the east highway out of Big Bear. Janice Gage's car was pushed off the shoulder of the road. She struck Lola Donne's coupe and both machines were wrecked.

Then the bombs had fallen. With eyes glazed Janice relived the horror. Only she, Lola, the boy Ted and his father survived. The Negro was hurt worse than any of them.

With the force of his personality alone the Negro kept them going throughout the night. The road above them was impassable for a mile or more. They had to climb through mesquite and manzanita. They might have returned to the highway above the slide, but by that time the Negro must have lost his sight. He led them by instinct, knowing they had to move constantly upward and feeling out their path by the inclination of the land. At dawn the women were too exhausted to go any farther. The Negro said he'd get help. In the pale light they saw his face and hands for the first time—the skin was in ribbons of burned flesh. And he still did not let them know he was blind. By sheer animal strength he managed to reach the highway, where we found him.

We lingered over the meal, under no compulsion of time. We had no appointments to keep. Hank Jenkins wandered in and joined us, bringing a half-empty fifth of liquor. Virginia Grant made a place for him at the table and piled his plate with food. Mrs. Bonhill made a pleasant ceremony of giving Jerry and me new clothes, which she had taken from a sporting goods shop.

Jerry and I went into a storage room behind the registration desk and put on the clothes. I winced when I felt the wool against my back. Bonhill laughed and said I had a touch of sunburn. As I went back to the lobby, I caught a glimpse of myself in a mirror on the door, and the man I saw was a stranger.

An American. The clothes symbolically completed my transformation, from Soviet paratrooper to American in eight hours. I belonged. And I understood, then, that America was not a nation, but a state of mind.

Cheryl Fineberg came and slid on the lounge between us. Bonhill tipped his cigar at a jaunty angle, grinning at her.

"I saw Willie Clapper go out right after dinner," she said, in a low voice. "He hasn't come back yet. I don't want to get everybody stirred up over nothing, but I think we should know what he's up to."

"We'll find him," Bonhill said.

Outside the hotel, he went east on the village street and I turned west. I saw Clapper a minute later, a hundred yards ahead of me. He slithered out of a sporting goods shop, jamming something into his coat pocket, and went into the drugstore where the Negro died.

As I ran toward the store, I saw him enter a telephone booth and drop a coin into the slot. After a moment, he began to jiggle the receiver hook. He didn't make his connection—fortunately, for it was a reasonable guess that he was trying to contact the invasion headquarters in Los Angeles. He met me at the door of the store. He shrugged noncommittally when I asked why he was telephoning.

Far away, on the road west of the village, we heard the hum of a motor. It stopped occasionally, and then moved toward us again.

"More refugees?" I asked.

Clapper threw back his handsome head and laughed uproariously. "Bonhill's car was the last one over the road last night before the fire closed the highway. Your pretty dream is finished, Lieutenant—and so soon, too. Academically, it would have been amusing to see just how much trash they could make you swallow." He put his hand on my shoulder and with the other pointed toward the sound of the approaching vehicle. "That will be our mutual friends from Los Angeles. If I couldn't get back to them, they had to come looking for me—obviously."

In blind rage I smashed my fist into his face—again and again, until he fell against the door and collapsed inside the shop.

We weren't licked. We couldn't be. And we had found a secret weapon, the stuff of the spirit that no arms could reach. I turned and ran back toward the hotel, signaling Jerry Bonhill with my hand. We had five minutes, perhaps less, before the Soviet car would be in the village. But we were Americans. That was all the time we needed.

V. The City—Saturday morning Dr. Stewart Roswell

CHEN PHIANG took us two blocks from the Dragen house to a garage apartment at the rear of a Chinese restaurant. The American planes were still raiding the harbor and above us the sky filled with cotton puffs from the exploding anti-aircraft shells.

We stumbled up the wooden stairway and Chen Phiang knocked on the door of the apartment—three times before it was opened. The soldier and a Chinese spoke rapidly in Cantonese and the door was flung wide to us. Chen Phiang put George Knight on a couch. Three women bent beside him, rubbing his hands and working pillows behind his head.

The man and Chen Phiang deluged each other with a flood of shrill Chinese. Their meeting was highly emotional. They threw their arms around each other—the small, dark-haired Chinese-American and the enormous man in the Communist uniform. Abruptly it was over. The soldier departed.

The Chinese shook my hand. His face still quivered with emotion; his fingers were trembling, warm with sweat. I told him who we were and how we had escaped from the Soviet headquarters. He glanced at George Knight—still unconscious—and said in a tone of deep humility,

"The Quaker teacher does an honor to my home."

"You know him?"

"Only his books. We are Buddhists, but all men of honor speak to the same end."

The three women brought a bottle of rubbing alcohol and washed Knight's face. The Quaker opened his eyes. Their kindness he accepted and understood at once, without words.

The Chinese told us his name was Lin Yeng. The three women were sisters, his wife Barbara and the beautiful teenager's Charlotte and Betty Sutong.

Lin Yeng could tell us very little about Chen Phiang, except that the soldier was a cousin, held for years in a Chinese concentration camp—or so they had always believed...

The next morning George Knight walked without my help into the front room of the apartment for breakfast—slowly, that's true, and dragging his right foot painfully, but under his own power. Considering how thoroughgoing Zergoff's education of the Quaker had been, Knight had made a remarkable recovery.

The Yengs had spread a round, teakwood table with bamboo mats and blue-glazed china. I saw the traditional, handleless teacups and the round rice bowls. But instead of tea, they gave us Coca-Cola to drink.

We heard footsteps on the stairs and Chen Phiang flung open the door. His uniform was soiled and disheveled. His flat, Oriental face was drawn tight with fatigue. He stood by our table, twisting his cap in his hand. Lin Yeng offered him food, but he turned it down.

"We'll take it all soon enough," he answered darkly. "Eat while you can." He said he had been on emergency duty all night—a search detail. General Zergoff had two hundred men combing the harbor area for Knight and me. The force was later increased to five hundred. Chen Phiang volunteered for the duty, to misdirect the search if it came too close to his cousin's apartment. His determination to save us had become the driving force of his being.

"The Russians will order a house to house search shortly," Chen Phiang declared. "Not this morning, perhaps. We still can't spare the manpower. But before that happens, I must get you away from the city."

"How?" Lin Yeng asked. "The roads are barricaded."

"There is a mountain place near here. I have heard talk of it. Some of our men were sent to look for a certain Dr. Clapper. If he is hidden so well, you might be, too."

I glanced at Knight. "Clapper does have a cabin somewhere between Running Springs and Big Bear."

"When the time comes," the Chinese soldier asked, "can you show me the proper road?"

"Yes."

"I will find transportation for us. Our submarines fought a naval battle last night. No one knows the outcome, but we expect an American task force to try a landing sometime today. They will be repulsed, naturally, but in the beginning there will be much confusion. That will be our opportunity to escape."

When the soldier turned to leave, Lin Yeng stopped him at the door. He said he had a gift of courtesy and he handed Chen Phiang a six-bottle carton of Coke. "In America, cousin, this is our national drink. A friend of America will use nothing else." He repeated very slowly, "Nothing else.

"Drink no water," Lin Yeng went on. "Go unwashed and unclean."

When Chen Phiang was gone, Barbara Yeng said anxiously, "I do hope he understood."

"I made it as plain as I dared," her husband replied.

"Not to me," I told them.

"When the milk collectors came during the night," Lin Yeng explained, "they told us. They were taking the warning to every American family. The Soviet bombers cut the irrigation canals that cross the desert, and the water still flowing to the city was affected by radiation. Before the week is out we'll have a water famine, but long before that every person who drinks the city water will undoubtedly suffer radiation poisoning. That means even more misery and a gruesome, painful death for those who consume the water."

VI. The Valley—Friday night Jerry Bonhill

THE plan was Yorovich's. He said the Russian car would head straight for the hotel as soon as the driver spotted Clapper's Cadillac. He wanted us to be concealed on both sides of the street, with rifles taken from a sporting goods store. We were to fire in front of the car and behind it, trying to make enough noise to suggest a large guerilla force.

In the meantime, from the second floor of the hotel, he would demand the surrender of the Soviets—in Russian, the parade-ground arrogance of a Russian officer. The psychological confusion should do the trick. Yorovich wanted Thatcher to have the submachine gun and to be posted with him in the second floor.

"If anything goes wrong," he said, "Thatcher, shoot to kill."

"I have one objection," Cheryl put in. "You should have the submachine gun, Boris. Pat would be more use to us down here."

The Russian blushed. His dark face was suddenly boyish and it was very easy for me to remember, then, that he was no older than I was. "I didn't think you'd want me—that is, if I had that weapon in my hands I could—"

"Give him the keys to the car," I told Pat.

Yorovich looked at me with inexpressible gratitude. He tried to say something, but all he was able to do was swallow—hard. Thatcher handed over the keys. The Russian ran into the street and unlocked the trunk compartment of the Cadillac. Three seconds later he was on his way up the stairs, the gun cradled in his arm.

"Let's snap to it," I said to the others. "Who's going outside with us?" They volunteered unanimously, even Jim Riley and the colored boy, Ted Fisher. I sent them into the kitchen of the coffee shop. I asked Hank Jenkins to stick with them—more to keep him off the streets than because I thought the kids needed watching. The rest of us filed through the sporting goods store, snatching up rifles and boxes of cartridges. An emergency seems to generate its own brand of efficiency. In less than two minutes we were concealed on both sides of the street.

The Soviet jeep entered the village. At an open window in the second floor of the hotel I saw Boris Yorovich stiffen and raise his gun to his shoulder. The jeep moved toward us. I counted four infantrymen, all of them armed with submachine guns. The two in back were standing, scanning the walks, their weapons cocked against their upper arms.

The jeep was in front of the hotel. In the stillness I heard the driver say very distinctly, "The Cadillac matches our description of Dr. Clapper's car." Afternoon sunlight, slanting over the hills, fell on his face. He was very young and very tired. The faint shadow of a blond beard was on his chin.

Then Yorovich's command echoed over the street. I saw the sudden fear and indecision in the young Russian's eyes. All four men looked up. Simultaneously the drugstore door banged open and Willie Clapper staggered out. They snapped their guns to their shoulder. "I'm Clapper!" he cried. "Don't shoot."

From our concealed positions we began to fire. Yorovich's voice barked again. Bullets from his submachine gun lashed across the hood of the jeep, shattering the windshield. The four men dropped their weapons and raised their hands. It was over.

No, it was just beginning. We swarmed around the car. Thatcher scooped up their weapons. I pushed the captives into the hotel.

We put the Russians on a lounge. Yorovich came down the steps and stood looking at them, the submachine gun draped carelessly over his arm. He grinned and said something in Russian. They stared at him, their eyes wide with fear. He spoke again and stiffly they reeled off their names and the other information he demanded.

Andrei Trenev.   Infantryman, eighteen, a small, fair-haired, blue-eyed boy conscripted from a Ukranian farm co-cooperative.

Vasili Shostovar.   Paratrooper, twenty, shallow-chested, beady-eyed, dark-haired, a mechanic from a Moscow implement depot; he had a two-year trade school education and appeared more sophisticated than the others.

Igor Morrenski.   Air-corps sergeant, seventeen, small and sturdy, with a broad, peasant face vaguely suggesting Mongol ancestry; he came from Stalingrad, where he had worked on a farm co-operative.

Feodor Psorkarian, Paratrooper, seventeen.   A tall, handsome, wild-eyed boy with an unruly shock of yellow hair and laughter on his lips.   A Cossack and proud of it. Of them all, perhaps the most adaptable personality.

Virginia Grant took over the job at that point. "I think, we'll get you some respectable clothes," she said.   "I disapprove of uniforms. Jerry, take them up to the men's shop and let them pick out something to wear." So I'd get her point, she repeated it firmly, "Let them do the choosing."

Shostovar protested like a good dialectician: we had no right to take their uniforms.

"If you want war on your terms, we take what we like," the teacher answered, lifting her rifle in a gesture that was unmistakable. "On ours, you have a choice. Make up your mind, Russian—that's the American way—but don't overlook all the consequences."

Yorovich and I took the four men to a sporting goods store, herding them carefully away from the racks of weapons. The Cossack took us at our word. We said he could take what he wanted and he did just that.   He squeezed his long, muscular legs into corduroy riding breeches, and he found a flame-colored, silk shirt. Around his waist he tied a broad, yellow scarf. He was delighted with what he saw when he examined himself in the full-length mirror. One by one the others stripped off their uniforms. Naked, they pawed through the display of clothing, whispering over the workmanship and awed by the abundance.

We fed the men at a table in the hotel lobby. None of us was able to eat so soon, except for Jim Riley and Ted Fisher. The two kids tore themselves away from their games long enough to plow through plates of beans and a quart of milk.

Willie Clapper had not come into the hotel when we were feeding the men. I didn't want to make an issue of it in front of them. Afterward Pat Thatcher and I tried to find him, without any luck. There were scores of places where he could have hidden in that deserted village. Pat and I were both certain he hadn't gone far.

"This could be dynamite," Pat told me.

I agreed with him. "I suppose Willie's planning to steal the Caddy or the jeep somehow and make tracks for L. A."

"Let him go, Jerry. In this set-up he's nothing but bait. They'll keep sending more men after him as long as he's here."

"It would be a hell of a lot worse if he got away. They'd send bombing planes, then, to wipe us out."

"They can smash up the village. We'd take to the hills; we'll have to sooner or later, in any case."

"You called him bait, Pat. Maybe that's not such a bad idea. Let the men come. We'll pull the same thing we did today."

He took a cigar from his pocket and jammed it into my

mouth. "It's your world, Jerry. If I'd been giving the orders this afternoon, they'd all be dead."

"Tonight we'll set up a watch in the hotel lobby. You and Yorovich and I."

"It looks as if we'll have to trust that Russian," Pat admitted. "You were right about him, Jerry."

"We'll give him the first watch, up to midnight. I'll take it from there until four. You cover the rest."

"You're biting off the tough part for yourself."

"I know that." I pulled on my cigar. "It's my world, you tell me. I'm ready to fight for it."

We had our community bedded down inside the hotel by eight o'clock. Cheryl and I rounded up Hank Jenkins; he was willing to call it a day when we let him take a bottle to his room. The four Russians we put into two storage rooms on the first floor back of the lobby. It seemed the safest place to keep them, since Thatcher, Yorovich and I were sleeping in the lobby. The men still had to be considered prisoners; I had no illusions about that.

Boris Yorovich shouldered a submachine gun and posted himself on the walk in front of the hotel. Pat Thatcher lay on a leather lounge under a woolen blanket. Moonlight slanted through a window on the old man's face; I saw the deep lines of exhaustion. Pat had given us everything he had. I began to understand why he had made such an effort to wake me up to my responsibilities. When Pat thrust the cigar between my teeth, he was resigning a leadership he hadn't the energy to hold. The act had been a symbol to him, perhaps more so than it was to me. When Pat was asleep, I walked to the front window and stood looking at the street. Fifty feet away I saw Yorovich's shadow, grotesquely lengthened by the angle of moonlight. The window was open. I heard the far cry of an animal in the forest above the village; I heard the wind in the pines.

And I felt terribly alone—a hollow, empty solitude. I realized how many decisions Pat had made for us. That job had become mine. I couldn't run back into my boyhood because I wasn't ready for anything else. I had to be ready. The Soviet invasion, whether I liked it or not, had made me a man.

I felt a hand on my shoulder. I turned and saw Cheryl in the darkness behind me. "I want to talk, Jerry," she whispered. "Let's go outside. We mustn't waken Pat."

I picked up a rifle and stuffed cartridges in my shirt pocket. "In case we meet Willie Clapper," I explained.

Cheryl and I passed Yorovich and walked toward the lake. The moon was very bright; stars blazed in the sky with the special brilliance given them by mountain heights. Cheryl drew me down on the pine needles beside her.

"I was so sure of it in my room, Jerry, but now—" She took my hand. Her fingers were hot and trembling. "I was thinking about my parents. Objectively. I haven't done that before. I knew I was alone. Everything is gone. We're never going back to it again."

"You grew up, Cheryl. We can't be school kids any more."

"Growing up—but even more than that, Jerry." She waved her hand toward the hills. "Out there is death and horror, a world falling apart. So little of it has touched us really, but I feel it like a terrible nightmare."

"We have to build a new world on—"

"I'm not talking about a world, Jerry." Her voice dropped to a whisper, like the gentle lapping of the lake water on the stony beach. "Tonight I became a woman, and a woman makes the abstract into something personal.

It's the way we are. The world is screaming death in my soul. Death; death! And inside of me is a cry of life—far stronger, far more real. Let the politicians tear the world down; a woman brings it alive again."

Suddenly she pressed her lips on mine. I felt a surge of excitement —like ice; like fire—blaze through my body. My arms tightened around her. "You're sure, Cheryl?" I asked. "You've made up your mind?"

"Not by the old standards, Jerry. Not love—the way my father had it in the movies he made."

We lay back on the knoll. The moon glowed above us, making a scarlet halo of her red hair. Her hands fumbled at my shirt. I felt the caress of her fingers on my chest...

Afterward Cheryl lay in my arms, the filmy web of her hair against my cheek.

She raised herself on her elbow and looked into my face, laughing softly. "You know, Jerry, I don't think I can truthfully say I picked you for looks." With her finger she traced the muscle football had built across my chest and belly. I felt no embarrassment, as I would have a week before.

The ecstasy burned in me again and I drew Cheryl against my breast.

And then our dream was shattered. Far away we heard a pistol shot and the high hum of an automobile motor. I pulled Cheryl to her feet and snatched up my rifle. We ran over the uneven ground toward the hotel.

VII. The City—Saturday morning Chen Phiang

I WALKED slowly away from my cousin's home, carrying his strange gift in my hands.

I stopped in an alleyway where none of our men could

see what I did, and I broke open a bottle by cracking the cap against a wall. The brown fluid was refreshing, sweet, in no way unpleasant. I drank it slowly, savoring the unfamiliar tang. This was a small thing, compared to the enormous crime I committed in rescuing the two intellectuals, yet the American drink had more meaning to me. It was a tangible act of defiance.

Nonetheless, it seemed an odd gift. Had my cousin understood the feeling of independence it would give me? Perhaps. But his eyes had said more than his words. "Drink no water." For some reason that was important.

As I walked back to my hotel I passed the Soviet headquarters house. The sidewall was broken and burned, but there was no other damage. General Zergoff was still stationed there, for the heavy guard was still around the house. A red ambulance stood in the street. The rear door was open. Three doctors in Russian uniforms were examining a man strapped to a wheeled stretcher.

I saw General Zergoff storm out of the house, trailing a retinue of clerks. The General looked at the man on the stretcher. He issued orders to the doctors, chopping the air with his hand in the assertive gesture so typical of the political commissar. The doctors bundled the man back into the ambulance. The vehicle shot down the boulevard, its siren screaming.

I went into a dark booth far at the back and I opened another bottle of Coke. I drank it slowly and again I had that feeling of wellbeing that came with honest defiance. I was one of them and I was not afraid.

Sound trucks came through the streets, blasting an official bulletin issued by the Soviet High Command. We were not to be alarmed by the large number of casualties. The men were not victims of an American poison—the

Fascist enemies of the people hadn't that much ingenuity—but of their own conscientiousness. Some troops during the night had come down too close to the bombed areas. They were suffering minor radioactive burns. But they would be given expert care by Soviet physicians, and each man was automatically awarded the Order of Lenin for his courage.

The confusion in the streets was the situation I wanted. As another red ambulance swung past the door, I suddenly realized how I could get my two intellectuals out of the city.

I left the saloon and ran toward my cousin's house.

VIII.   The Valley—Saturday morning. Jerry Bonhill

BORIS YOROVICH lay on the walk, blood spilling over his shirt from a bullet wound in his shoulder. The Cadillac was gone. I bent over the Russian. "Clapper!" he whispered. He pointed weakly toward the door of the hotel.

"Take care of him, Cheryl," I snapped. She nodded.

In the lobby I groped for the matches and lighted the oil lamp we had left as an emergency light on the registration desk. I saw Pat Thatcher. His skull was smashed. His shirt had been ripped open in Clapper's eagerness to get the keys to the Cadillac.

Numbly I pulled the blanket over Pat's face. For a moment I was paralyzed by grief. Thatcher's murder had more meaning to me than the death of my own father.

I heard voices in the upper hall and I shook the weight of grief from my mind. One of the storage room doors burst open and Feodor Psorkarian hobbled across the threshold. The Cossack's feet and hands were tied. He was working his head furiously to free himself from the yellow scarf gagging him. I cut him free. He cried his excited, Russian anger. Then, remembering, I wouldn't understand him, he said in almost equally chaotic English,

"After him we go! That spy; that saboteur! He came; he threatened—like the secret police. Always the fear. Always the guns!" The Cossack pulled me toward the door. "Our jeep. You have the keys, my American friend. We still have time to stop them!"

I looked in his eyes. What I saw made my decision for me. I threw him my rifle. "O.K., Cossack, let's go."

We leaped into the jeep. I drove. Psorkarian steadied my rifle on the hood while he held his eye on the road ahead of us.

He was calm enough then to give a coherent picture of what had happened. Willie Clapper broke into the storage room, which the Cossack shared with Andrei Trenev. Clapper was armed with a pistol he had stolen from a village sporting goods shop that afternoon. He asked their help to escape. The Cossack refused.

After persuasion failed, Clapper tried threats. He said he would turn all the prisoners over to the secret police, but if the Cossack and Trenev would help him he promised them leniency. The Cossack had heard Russian promises before; he wasn't buying any. Trenev, of course, was frightened into obedience. He stood at attention and saluted Clapper. Psorkarian swung his fist at Trenev, but Clapper struck the Cossack with the handle of his pistol.

We were two hundred yards behind the Cadillac when Clapper first spotted us. Andrei Trenev opened fire with his rifle. Feodor Psorkarian adjusted his sights casually. He muttered, "try to outrun a Cossack, will you?" He took deliberate aim and fired. The rear window of the Cadillac shattered.

He fired twice in rapid succession. Both rear tires on the Cadillac blew. The car lurched into the embankment, slid along the granite, and spun off the highway. We heard the crash of rending metal and glass as I jammed on the brakes.

The wreckage lay precariously suspended on a narrow ledge forty feet below the road. We heard no sound except the slow turning of a wheel suspended in space. The Cossack and I climbed down the rocks. Clapper was dead, the post of the steering column rammed like a lance through his chest. Andrei Trenev lay face up on the ledge, his right leg bent grotesquely beneath him. He was conscious; his face was twisted with pain and terror.

The Cossack stood over him, holding the rifle like a club. "Shall I finish him?"

"No!" I threw the back of my arm against his wrist. In his surprise Psorkarian almost lost his balance. "We'll take him back to the village."

We made a stretcher of our shirts and carried him back to the jeep. There was flask of vodka in the pocket; Psorkarian tipped it against Trenev's lips and the pain washed slowly out of his eyes. The fear went with it.

"You're helping me," the boy whispered.

It was close to midnight when we returned to the hotel. We carried Trenev into the lobby and lay him on a lounge. The others were all waiting for us. Boris Yorovich sat propped in a chair, his shoulder wrapped with gauze. Janice Gage was beside him, holding his hand.

Hank said he would sit up with his patients. This was important for the restoration of his ego.

The next morning we buried Pat Thatcher beside the

Negro's grave, on the knoll overlooking the lake.

We were all there; even Andrei Trenev had been carried to the knoll on a stretcher. I was acutely aware of my own position. Subtly each of them acknowledged my leadership, the choice Pat had made. They were watching me, wondering if I could carry it off. I knew that, too. A kid of nineteen!—I felt one moment of cold panic, and Cheryl's hand was in mine and I was a man again.

In dead silence I shook the hand of each of the Russians. I turned very deliberately and, with Cheryl beside me, walked back toward the hotel.

"Was that wise?" she asked. "So soon?"

"There's nothing else we can do, Cheryl. Pat told me Clapper was bait as long as we kept him here. He's dead; we can't get rid of him, now. The Russians will keep sending men after him. We have to trust the ones we have. A military stand is ridiculous."

And we didn't have long to wait. Less than half an hour after the others returned to the hotel, we heard a motor on the road east of the village. I told Yorovich to give our Russians their submachine guns; we'd try the same type of ambush that had worked so successfully the day before.

I heard the truck motor. I heard Yorovich's shout and the burst of gunfire. A confusion of voices. More gunfire. Then silence. Slow footsteps on the marble tile of the lobby. Feodor Psorkarian stood at the coffee shop door. He held the submachine gun at an angle in his hand. Smoke still curled from the barrel. Blood trickled from a wound in his arm.

"We didn't do this as neatly as you did, Jerry," he said. "Five we killed; only nine surrendered."

"And our people?"

"Just this scratch." He touched his wound negligently.

"Andrei fought like a demon.

"There's something else, Jerry. Three of the prisoners—and I'll swear not a bullet touched them—are lying in the road spitting up blood. A couple of others look damn sick."

I ran toward the street. "Where's Hank Jenkins?"

"He's already out there."

IX. The Valley—Saturday afternoon. Dr. Stewart Roswell

BEFORE noon on the second day of the war George Knight and I escaped Los Angeles. Chen Phiang developed an amazing ingenuity.

Originally, the Communist soldier planned to take only Knight and myself out of Los Angeles. But Lin Yeng's family went with us as well. "By tomorrow this will be a city of death. We have no reason to stay," Lin said.

Six of us crowded into the body of the panel truck. It was hot and it became unbearably stuffy.

We remained locked in the back of the truck until we reached the Arrowhead highway at Running Springs. Chen Phiang got out, then, and opened the rear door. "I think there will be no more guard posts," he said. "But perhaps it is not wise to stop here. I do not know your mountains."

"By tomorrow it won't matter," Lin Yeng told him.

"The sickness?" his cousin asked. "Is it truly an American poison or—"

"A poison, yes. But it's something they did to themselves." Lin Yeng described the effect of radiation on the city water supply. The Chinese soldier grimaced. He looked at his uniform, wiping his hands over the rough cloth. Suddenly he ripped off the tunic and flung it away.

He kicked off his boots and removed the paratrooper's trousers. He stood naked on the deserted road, a powerful man having the muscular grace of a tiger. With his uniform gone, I seemed to see his face for the first time— the handsome, strongly intelligent face of a boy. His hair was shaved close. His eyes glowed with the hope of youth—the same idealism I had seen in my classrooms for as long as I had been teaching.

The Orientals did not have our western mores about modesty, and the Chinese family was undisturbed by what Chen Phiang had done.

Knight got out of the truck and hobbled a short distance, exercising his muscles. But I saw that it was very painful to him. His face went white and it was beaded with sweat. I helped him back to the truck. He leaned against the door, breathing hard.

"Stewart," he said, "I told you this catastrophe gives us a magnificent opportunity. We mustn't lose it."

"Not all of us, I'm afraid, are going to see it quite the way you do."

"If I could only persuade people to know the good that is in their own hearts! If I could talk to them—" He put his hand on my arm. "By tomorrow, Stewart, the troops in Los Angeles will be at our mercy. Sick men dying in agony. There are two things our people could do. We could take revenge. We could kill them all. But suppose for the first time in human history we met force and hatred with love!"

"You might pull off your miracle, Knight, if you could speak to every individual in Los Angeles as you have to me."

Chen Phiang appeared wearing jeans and a plaid shirt. Back in the truck Lin Yeng and I rode in front with Chen, to give the others more room. Lin wanted us to drive as far as Big Bear; since it was larger than any other mountain resort, he thought we might have a chance of finding people there.

Once we stopped to round up some refugees. It was three hours before we found them all and helped them back to the truck.

Because we had stopped so long on the road, it was five o'clock in the afternoon—Saturday, the second day of the war—before our panel truck entered the village of Big Bear. A tall, broad-shouldered boy of nineteen—with the penetrating gaze of a man; a frightening kind of maturity—met us in front of the hotel. His name was Jerry Bonhill.

X. *The Valley—Sunday night Jerry Bonhill.*

THE water, as cold as a mountain spring, lashed over my body from the showerhead. Clean water, good water: we had it in our valley, while the city below the mountain stank with poison and death.

In the adjoining bedroom I heard static from my portable radio, and suddenly the clear, quiet voice of George Knight. It was nearly dusk Sunday night, the third day of the war. For twelve hours the Quaker had been broadcasting from the transmitter in the frame building behind Canster's appliance shop.

Cheryl banged on the bathroom door. "They have it going again, Jerry!"

I grabbed a towel from the rack and went into the bedroom, mopping off the cold water while I listened to the broadcast. The Quaker's patient, reasoned plea came in prefectly. I hoped to God the reception was as clear in Los Angeles.

Cheryl lay on the bed, her head close to the radio. She

looked at my nakedness and smiled like a vixen.

Suddenly her lips were on mine, liquid and yielding. I felt the pulsing fire leap in my blood. I saw the sensuous woman triumphant in her eyes.

"You devil," I laughed. "When I want to talk seriously—"

"There's a time for talking, my love, and a time for—"

She gasped as I pulled her down on the bed beside me.

Afterward, Cheryl lay pressed against my side, her eyes closed and a smile on her lips. I relaxed in the peace and the stillness of our love. I became aware again of George Knight's voice coming from the speaker of my portable.

The third day of the war, and we knew that the collapse of civilization was complete. Nothing could hold back the chaos. The stench of death in Los Angeles was a mirror held up to the face of a ruined planet. Few people had died in the original bombings; the cities had been organized to meet that emergency, but no organization could cope with what followed—a network of continental rivers, steeped in radioactive poison and carrying the sickness everywhere.

We had one way we could help—and only one: George Knight's plea to the people of Los Angeles.

Cheryl stirred and opened her eyes. She leaned across my chest to turn down the radio.

"What happens, Jerry, if they don't listen to him?"

"They'll kill a good many of the Russians, and the Russians will retaliate."

"Our world shrinks to the size of a mountain valley."

"Enough—we have each other."

"You and I, Jerry—we're not twenty yet, and the others look to us—" She drew in her breath sharply.

"Why, Jerry? Why you and me? Couldn't someone

else—"

"We can't dodge it."

I pulled on my shirt. Cheryl got up and put her arm around my shoulder. "I'm beginning to see you now, Jerry, as Pat did."

I cracked her rear with the palm of my hand.

"A man, Jerry. That's all it takes—but suddenly I realize how much courage it takes to be a human being."

Through the window behind her I saw the windmill lifts of a helicopter whirring against the red sky.

"The Soviets are back," I said to Cheryl, pointing toward the ship. "Run over to the lodge and tell the others to break out the guns. I'm going down to the hospital after Psorkarian. The Cossack might just be able to knock down the 'copter with a submachine gun."

"Be careful, Jerry."

I left the cabin and ran toward the hotel. The ship was moving toward us cautiously; the pilot wasn't taking any unnecessary risks, and he didn't know how well armed we might be. I assumed they were still after Clapper; no other possibility occurred to me.

On the village street, half a block from the hotel, I saw Boris Yorovich and Janice Gage, walking arm in arm. Naturally, they hadn't seen the Russian ship. They were too immersed in each other. I jerked them back to reality; Yorovich said he would get Psorkarian.

"George Knight's all right?" I asked.

"The transmitter's working fine; Janice and I came up for dinner. We were on our way back—"

"Join him as soon as you can; I don't like to leave him alone."

They ran toward the hotel. I returned to the lodge beside the lake; most of our weapons were there. As I sprinted over the hill, I saw a parachutist descending twenty feet above me. The paratrooper had a submachine gun in his hand.

The man came down close to me. I sprang as his feet touched the ground. I had no time to reach the lodge and arm myself. The man was a giant, a human machine of flesh and bone driven by the hypnotic opiate of hatred.

Screaming in animal fury, he swung his submachine gun toward me. I kicked upward against the barrel. The hail of bullets spattered the trees above my head. I kicked again and I saw his grip loosen; I jerked the gun from his hands. He lunged at me, swinging his arms like bear claws. I clipped his jaw with my knuckles. Physically the blow rocked him back on his heels, but he seemed unaware of the pain.

He reached for my feet and dragged me down. His clawing hands found my throat. I fought to break the grip, hammering my fists into his jaw. The face was a bleeding pulp before his fingers slid away and I was able to breathe again.

I stood up. A clanging echo sang in my ears. I heard more gunfire, from another direction, and after a moment I located it: the transmitter! The objective of this raid had not been Willie Clapper, but George Knight.

I snatched up the paratrooper's submachine gun, where it had fallen, and I ran toward the village. I came toward the appliance shop from the east. West of the transmitter I saw occasional spurts of gunfire in the shadows.

Two men were leaving the transmission shack. In the pale light inside the building I saw George Knight lying back in his chair. He was dead. They had beaten the gentle Quaker to death with the butts of their weapons. The two men were stringing wires from an explosive charge they had left in the building.

I raised my gun and fired. They died screaming, as the bullets ripped open their skulls. Four other paratroopers, who had been holding off Yorovich and Psorkarian, sprang up at the sound of the shots. I had no shelter. Bullets from their guns tore the soft earth toward me. I squeezed the trigger of the submachine gun; simultaneously Yorovich and the Cossack moved out of hiding. The four men died in our crossfire.

Blood soaked the sleeve of my left arm. My fingers felt numb, with a kind of remote and impersonal pain. Yorovich and Psorkarian loomed out of the shadows.

We ran along the village street in the darkness. The sky above us was red with the last light of the dying sun.

XI. *The Valley—Monday afternoon Jerry Bonhill*

AFTER we buried Knight, we made fifteen graves at another part of the lakeshore for the nameless men who had died during the Soviet air attack. There were no survivors.

The Soviet attack made it clear that the broadcasts were having some effect in the city. Otherwise, the Russians would not have traced the transmitter and tried to destroy it. Stewart Roswell warned me not to read too much into that, however. "General Zergoff has a bitter, personal conflict with Knight. He would send his whole force up here, if he thought he could find Knight."

It was late in the morning before I had an opportunity to examine the helicopter.

I asked Vasili Shostovar to go with me. He had been a mechanic in Moscow and, better than any of us, he would be able to judge what repairs had to be made. The thin, swarthy man had begun to modify his clothing and he looked less like a slum kid in uniform. He made no more oblique references to party discipline. He had joined us in the ambush of the second Soviet car; that made him one of us, and I accepted it. But there was no feeling of friendship between us, none of the honest affection I felt for the Cossack and Morrenski—yes, even Andrei Trenev, who had attempted to help Willie Clapper escape.

The Russian looked over the motor carefully.

"She's as good as new, Bonhill." His words were vaguely slurred; on his breath I caught the sour odor of liquor.

"What about the fuel?" I asked.

He glanced into the cabin. "Better than half a tank."

"Could we use gasoline from the village service stations?"

"I doubt it. But Psorkarian says there's an airport in the eastern part of the valley; you ought to find some aviation fuel there."

"Do you know how to fly?"

"No. Grennig, the Russian, does."

Karl Grennig was twenty-four, as large as I am and perhaps thirty pounds heavier—all of it hard muscle. He had the blond, Nordic good looks, which the Germans had once built into a maniac's cult of war.

"You want to use the 'copter?" Grennig asked.

"Possibly."

"The Doc says I'll be up and around by tomorrow. Where do you want to go—" He hesitated for a moment before he added, with an ingenuous smile, "—Commander?"

"We've no use for titles. My name is Bonhill."

186

"Sorry, sir. You'll have to—"

"The 'sir,' too. We're not a military camp."

"It's a habit the Communists taught us. Personally, I've always hated it." When Karl Grennig got the point, he jumped on the bandwagon fast enough. But the transition was a nasty thing to watch. Grennig was suddenly buddy-buddy with me. "I've got news for you, Bonhill, you may not have picked it up, yet. The Red troop transports won't be coming in any more; maybe they've already stopped."

"Roswell tells me they have landings scheduled for a week. What happened?"

"I picked up the gossip at headquarters. They're keeping this under wraps as long as they can. It's a breakdown in the distribution of supplies to the Siberian bases. Primarily food and fuel."

"How many Communist troops are in Los Angeles now, Grennig?"

"Two hundred thousand. A quarter of a million at most. The whole Red machine has broken down in Europe and Asia. The after-effects of the bombing are worse than anyone expected. The Politburo is finished…"

Los Angeles was the only metropolitan area, which had a chance of surviving. That was the assumption we had to make. More and more I realized how fundamental Knight's message was. The invading army was all that remained of the enemy, and the city was all of America that had escaped the disaster. Here, flung together, were the two halves of our world, the last fragments of the old civilization. Here they had to find peace; they had to survive. In this city—if they listened to Knight—we could build tomorrow.

If they listened to George Knight. They had to hear the Quaker's message and they had to believe in it. It was the only chance.

XII. The City—Tuesday, The Fifth day. Jerry Bonhill

TUESDAY afternoon, the fifth day of the war, I went back to Los Angeles with Stewart Roswell. Grennig piloted our helicopter.

I wore two revolvers belted to my jeans and I carried a rifle. But I made sure Grennig carried no arms.

I offered Roswell a rifle, but he pushed it aside. "I've never shot a gun in my life, Jerry."

"It's time you started learning."

He smiled. "Even to build a society based on love?"

"Idealism with teeth in it." I pushed the weapon in his hands; he took it reluctantly. "A man has to survive before he can build."

Grennig brought the 'copter low over San Bernardino and we saw the first stark evidence of the fighting. The downtown district of the suburb was a burned-out ruin. Residential streets had been bombed indiscriminately, but many of the houses were still standing.

As we moved closer to Los Angeles, the devastation became worse.

The industrial district and the heart of the city were an unrecognizable shambles.

Roswell said, "They were expecting a naval attack when Knight and I left the city."

"That must have been the heavy guns we heard yesterday."

Roswell's face was white; beads of sweat stood on his lips. "It looks as if the navy made a successful landing. The Russians were trapped. They used gas and destroyed everything—to hold the territory they had taken."

Karl Grennig broke in, "Our boys are supposed to

have—I mean to say, the Communists are supposed to have very effective chemical weapons. A couple of dozen bombs dropped from the air would wipe out the city."

At Roswell's request we flew north from the harbor and landed on the beach. The homes along the ocean front boulevard were undamaged. Roswell picked up the rifle I had given him.

"Idealism with teeth to it," he muttered. "I'm going to need this after all, Jerry."

He jumped from the cabin, landing on the soft warm sand. "One man would give the order to destroy the city; and one man would manage to survive, if all the world died. Don't wait for me. I don't think I'll be back."

He strode toward the wooden stairs leading from the beach to the top of the bluff. I called after him, "Where the hell're you going, Roswell?"

He plodded on without answering. I motioned Grennig toward the cabin door. His face paled. "It's suicide, Bonhill! There are still some Soviet troops around up there. We don't stand a chance."

"Then we have to bring Roswell back, don't we?"

When Grennig and I reached the boulevard, Roswell was on the walk in front of a large, pseudo-Spanish mansion. I knew the house. It belonged to Marvin Dragen III.

Soviet soldiers lay dead on the boulevard, their guns still clutched in their hands. These were the diehards; they had won the city of the dead—and died themselves. None of the men was wearing a mask. Obviously they hadn't known the gas was to be used.

I saw him, then, as the door of the Dragen house swung open. A tall, Soviet General in full dress uniform. The Order of Lenin on his breast caught and held the glint of the afternoon sun. He was wearing a gas mask that hid his face and deprived him of his only human resemblance.

A god of war gone mad, for the danger from the gas had long since gone. He held a submachine gun in his hand. He aimed it at Stewart Roswell.

"Zergoff," Roswell whispered.

The Russian squeezed the trigger before I had time to fire. The hammer of Zergoff's weapon fell on an empty chamber.

"I held the beachhead," the Russian said proudly, his voice muffled by the mask. "Not even the American navy could throw me out."

"You did this?" Roswell asked. "You killed them all?"

Roswell fumbled with his rifle. But he did not fire. He turned away and walked toward Grennig and me, staggering like a drunken man. Zergoff continued to fire.

"Let him die in his own way," Roswell said, "in his dead city. Pray God give him just one minute of sanity before it's over! Let him smell the stench of death and see the ruins; let him know the thing he's done; let him judge his own inhumanity. That's hell enough for any man."

Roswell gripped my arm. He was gasping for breath and I saw tears in his eyes.

Part Three
The First Two Years,
Jerry Bonhill

I. The Valley—Tuesday evening, The Fifth Day

THIS was our physical world—fourteen men and two boys; twelve women and a Mexican child of fourteen. Five of them were Chinese; two were Negro; two Indians; four Russians, a German and an Italian. Catholics, Jews, Protestants, Hindus, Buddhists. The races of man; the nations of man; the faiths of man.

I told them briefly what we had seen in Los Angeles. I said they were free to go back to the dead city and live with the dead, scavenging food in the ruins.

I saw dismay on their faces, the shadow of the lonely horror. I went on quickly to suggest a general plan of survival.

I said we would begin with an inventory of our resources—the tools, the canned food, the clothing, the gasoline, the hunting guns, the shells, which were available in the village. We would move everything into the largest market and use it as a warehouse. Until we worked out a system of replacements, nothing was to be taken out of that warehouse except on my written order. I asked Lin Yeng and his wife to manage the warehouse for us—to classify the supplies and to set up an accounting system for all withdrawals.

From the back of the room Vasili Shostovar spoke up. "Highhanded is the word for it. Suppose we don't want to play your game, Bonhill?"

I answered quietly, "You don't have to stay in the

valley."

Shostovar snorted. "All this fine talk of yours about your American way of life! Right now you're setting up Communism. Did we vote on any of this? Did we elect you to—"

Psorkarian sprang up, his face angry in the white glare of the lantern. "Then we'll hold an election. We'll put Jerry in office."

I knew the Cossack would get a majority, but that sort of formal procedure was the last thing I wanted. "These are only emergency measures," I told him. "Anyone of you would suggest exactly the same things."

I set up a communal dining system for all of us in the lodge, because that made it easier to use our food efficiently. I asked seven women to do the kitchen chores—Mom, the Sutong sisters, and three of the women Chen Phiang had picked up on the road. Since the supply of fresh food was our most immediate problem, I suggested that we begin farming operations at once.

Morrenski said, in his plodding way, "I have seen seed packets in the stores here. We can use them for the first planting."

"For our second season, we'll take seeds from this year's crop," Trenev added.

I assigned Chen Phiang, Shostovar, Grennig and Giorgio Leopardi to work with Morrenski and Trenev, and I threw in the three kids as well—Jim Riley, Ted Fisher and Carlota Porra. It would do them good to work in the summer sun, and they needed to feel that they were doing their part.

Our only source of fresh meat would be the game we shot. I appointed Boris Yorovich and Feodor Psorkarian our community hunters. It was logical, then, to give them control of our firearms. In the shadow government I had to make, the two men would be the police power.

We had one more interruption from Shostovar. "You're organizing a nice little dictatorship, Bonhill; I hope the rest of these fools understand that."

"An emergency economy," I repeated patiently.

"Communism, and we may as well face it. You arbitrarily assign us work. You give us no choice. You—"

"You make the choice if you stay in the valley," I reminded him for a second time. "We've all had our fill of arguments over words, Shostovar. There's one big difference between what we're doing and the police state you came from. Here you aren't afraid to say what you think. You didn't hesitate to call me a dictator a minute ago. You know you can talk as much as you like and nothing's going to happen to you."

The meeting broke up after dark.

"This is the beginning, isn't it?" Cheryl asked me as we crossed the hill.

"We'll survive. If we have faith in ourselves, our world will never die."

Faith: that fundamental human need. I had organized the material resources of the valley, but I had provided nothing to satisfy man's inner soul. I mulled that over as I showered and dressed for dinner.

It was the problem of formal religion, and I was afraid of it—afraid of the potential conflict it involved. Each man has his own god. A sincere faith often comes hand in hand with a fanatic will to convert others. We had such a jumble of orthodoxies in our valley, faith itself might one day smash our new world into dust.

My solution to the problem crystalized around the feeling each of us had for George Knight. I proposed it that night at dinner in the lodge.

The knoll where Knight and Thatcher and the Negro were buried I made our community place of worship—a church without walls and without ritual, a church for all men open to the face of God.

The idea was a dud at first. The conventions of the dead world passed slowly. Yet, in time, we accepted the knoll as a commonplace part of our lives.

It was a slow-working miracle performed by the gentle persuasion of a Quaker who was dead. It made us see the essential spirit of all our gods.

It was our first real vision of George Knight's new world.

II. *Outside the Valley—July, The First Year*

IN JULY I made my first expedition away from the valley. By that time our economy was functioning without a hitch. We were farming more than fifty acres of the rich, black soil; the corn was already waist high.

Eight times Chen Phiang and Feodor Psorkarian drove to the city, foraging for equipment and supplies we had not found in the village. By their third trip they had brought back two enormous vans, and enough drums of diesel fuel to keep the trucks running for years.

They pillaged every library that had escaped the fire. Stewart Roswell classified the books and shelved them in the village high school. Eventually we had more than two hundred thousand volumes. Reading became one of our regular leisure activities.

That summer was an idyll for us all. We faced no hardship and no privation; none of us had any really difficult work to do. Four or five hours a day was the longest time anyone worked on the farm. An idyll in the hot, mountain sun.

By the beginning of July ten couples had moved into cottages along the lake. Yorovich was living with Janice Gage and Psorkarian had taken Lola Donne—or perhaps it was the other way around.

A kind of wedding ceremony gradually developed. At a meal in the lodge, when we were all together, both the man and the woman formally announced their intention to live with each other. They asked me to assign them a cabin of their own.

Chen Phiang married Charlotte Sutong. Charlotte's sister, Betty, was living with the most adaptable of the two Indians, Palra Rubhai.

Giorgio Leopardi married Helen White, a fragile, serious, intelligent girl very much like himself. Conscientious in the ritual of his church, Leopardi went through an intense, inner conflict before he made up his mind. We had no ordained priest to perform the sacrament of marriage and no likelihood of finding any.

Igor Morrenski, plodding, slowwitted, and conscientious, took a wife amazingly different from himself. Emily Marsh, not yet twenty, was by far the most attractive of the five refugees the Yengs had brought in. She was a goddess for him to worship.

Only Karl Grennig and Vasili Shostovar had not taken wives. Except for Mom and Virginia Grant, both in their sixties, and Carlota Porra, not yet fourteen, we had no other unattached women in the valley. Potentially it could become an explosive situation. The least reliable men in our community were excluded from something the rest of us shared.

In order to head off that conflict, I tried to find other

refugees to bring to the valley. During July Grennig taught me to fly the helicopter; he gave the same instruction to Psorkarian, because I was taking the Cossack with me. I needed his quick wit and very possibly his accurate trigger finger. Our shadow government I left to Stewart Roswell and Boris Yorovich.

We flew north first, beyond the Techachapis. The San Joaquin Valley was a wasteland. Three or more of the big bombs had fallen there—perhaps because Soviet bombers had been shot down over the valley, or the San Joaquin may have been a tactical Soviet target. In either case, the results were the same.

Farther north the devastation was worse. The bombs in the San Francisco area had changed the face of the map. A forty-mile chunk of the peninsula had disappeared; the bay was open to the sea. A tiny, smooth-domed island, washed by a heavy sea, marked the point where the city had been. Bombs had ripped open an inland lake farther west in the bed of the Sacramento River.

Two hundred miles north of the state capital we saw our first people, an enormous refugee camp sprawling on the flat, hot plain near Shasta Dam. Shock waves had cracked open the dam and water trickled in scores of tiny streams across the plain. Tents, shacks jerrybuilt from cardboard containers, and automobiles crowded the banks of the streams. We skimmed low over the camp, and we smelled the stench of death. The bodies, huddled by the water, were bloated and black with decay. Buzzards picked at the white skulls; coyotes walked the ruins.

We followed the Sierra range south. On the Feather River we spotted a small camp, but it was deserted. Two dozen automobiles were parked by stone fire rings. Clothing, cots, and empty food cartons were scattered on the ground, perhaps by foraging bears. Water from a recent rain lay in the open fire beds, indicating that the people had been gone for some days.

At dusk we were over Tahoe. The forests and the resorts on the east shore of the lake had burned in a fire started by the bomb that flattened Reno. The fire had cut a crescent path around Emerald Bay. We saw three cars in the State Park which overlook the bay. Ten people were sprawled grotesquely on the ground. A child was crawling in the dust.

We brought the helicopter down in the clearing. The child screamed when she saw us and tried to run. I caught her. She clawed at my face with her hands and pounded her fists against my chest.

"Take it easy, kid; we want to help you."

"You have guns! You kill people!" She couldn't have been more than four. Her voice still had a trace of a childish lisp. We finally quieted her hysteria by giving her food. She was ravenously hungry; she ate like a starving animal.

While I still held her in my arms, Psorkarian and I crossed the clearing and examined the bodies. The adults had been shot. The appearance of the camp suggested a pitched battle. I asked the girl what had happened.

"They came and they talked to my Daddy and then they began to shoot." With her dirty hands she stuffed more crackers into her mouth.

"Who came, kid?"

"The bad men. They said they would give Daddy money for our food, and he wouldn't take it."

"Where are the men now, do you know?"

"In the woods." She pointed vaguely. "Do you have anything else to eat?"

"All you can hold. Let's get you cleaned up first."

"The picture's clear enough," the Cossack said. "Some of the survivors die of radiation; the rest fight it out over the scraps of food that are left."

"In less than two months we've become savages."

"Starvation, Jerry, has one law —survival."

A shot echoed from the trees and a bullet sang across the fire ring. The child began to scream again. The Cossack fired his rifle into the darkness. I grabbed the girl and ran toward the helicopter. Bullets slashed the earth close to my feet. I threw the child into the back of the cabin and snatched up the submachine gun, spraying the trees with lead. I heard a shrill cry and a man's voice cursing.

Psorkarian pushed past me into the ship. I fired another round as he started the motor. I leaped into the cabin and the helicopter rose slowly. I saw a mob of men and women crowding into the clearing, firing up at us. I swept them with bullets from the machine gun.

As our ship cleared the pines, Psorkarian said, "They thought we had food—or maybe they wanted the 'copter." I saw him smile. "And I was just about to suggest that this would be a peaceful place to spend the night. Seems to me, we'll be safer down in the valley with the dead."

Safer with the dead. We didn't have to worry about their integrity or their respect. Only the dead would understand George Knight's dream. The living? In another generation they would be dancing war chants around a witch doctor's ceremonial campfire.

III. The Valley—Christmas, The First Year

"You were right, Jerry," Cheryl said. "It does sound pretty."

I stooped and kissed the back of her neck as I carried

another log to the fire. We were in our cabin dressing. From the lodge next door we could hear the piano, and the voices singing carols. It was Christmas Eve, our first winter in the valley. Snow lay four feet deep on the ground. The full moon, riding low above the ridge, transformed our tiny world into a fairyland.

The traditional Christmas was entirely my idea. My shadow government had been against it. Yorovich and the Cossack because they knew nothing about the holiday; Cheryl because it was a Christian festival excluding other faiths.

I knew if I turned the arrangements over to Mom that I'd get exactly the thing I had in mind. Mom was a storehouse for superficialities. She gave us an innocuous holiday of genial good fellowship—a holiday for kids.

We had fourteen of them in the valley that Christmas, ranging in age from four to fourteen. After our first exploration north to Tahoe, Psorkarian and I made six more helicopter hops out of the valley before the snows began. Each time we were able to rescue orphaned children and bring them back with us.

The children gave me a kind of hope again. They would keep our new world alive, if we failed.

The Cossack and I traveled as far away from our valley as Utah and the northern states of Mexico. We had seen so much desolation, so much death, we had become immune to it. People had survived, yes—but fewer than we would have guessed—and sometimes we spotted roving bands on the earth below us. They had become almost literally savage tribes —barbarians, thinly veneered with the skills of civilization and the mores of sophistication.

Twice the Cossack and I tried to talk with small groups.

They respected us because we were better armed; but they had no respect for what we had to say.

One group gladly traded us two small children for a case of canned food. Even the mothers shed no tears. They had a new system of values built on expediency, survival, and a reasonably full belly.

Cheryl got up from the dresser, pushing her new shirt— a bright, flannel plaid—into her jeans. Mom had insisted on having gifts to go with her kind of Christmas, and I authorized Lin Yeng to issue new clothes for all of us from the warehouse.

"How do I look?" Cheryl asked.

"The way a wife should." I grinned and ran my hand over the swelling mound of her abdomen.

She kissed me. "Jerry, he's going to be born in a good world."

"Of course, we're making exactly—"

"I know how you've felt since that first trip out, when you brought back little Nancy Watson. You haven't talked about it, but there isn't much you can hide from me."

"It's all right now, Cheryl. I wanted to do too much too fast; I realize that."

"Do you, Jerry? Sometimes I see the sadness and the frustration in your eyes and I—" She looked into my face. "You need the symbolism of Christmas; we all do. Perhaps that's why you insisted upon it the way you did." She kissed me long and ardently and her lips murmured, "Merry Christmas, Jerry."

We crossed the snow to the lodge, using the snowshoes Igor Morrenski had made us out of pine and strips of deer hide. Most of the others were there ahead of us. I had worked late that afternoon in the corral, building a stall roof broken by the weight of snow. Three long tables were set close together in front of the fire. Mom had decorated them with pinecones and fir boughs. She had found some red and green candles in the warehouse. The children sat together at one table, laughing and whispering together and eyeing the packages under the tree.

As much as possible we kept the children together, to build in their minds an instinctive pattern of mutual sharing. Yet a family discipline was necessary, too; each of them had a permanent home in one of the lakeside cottages.

The women brought in the food from the lodge kitchen—three large roasts of deer meat, vegetables canned from our own fields, cranberries withdrawn from the warehouse, hot pumpkin pies with a strange, cracker-like crust made from ground cornmeal and our own butter. Except for salt and sugar and luxury items, we had made ourselves independent of the canned food in the village.

When our Christmas Eve dinner was finished, Mom brought in the punchbowl. I had let her have liquor to make the eggnog, which she considered fundamental to the holiday.

Mom filled cups for all the adults. She hesitated when she came to me. At home she always made me a special, "stickless" concoction—even after I had started in college, and had gone on the usual freshman-year bender. Finally she filled a cup half full. "You're—you're living with a woman now, Jerry; I guess it's all right."

She never called it marriage.

I noticed that Vasili Shostovar and Karl Grennig came back to the punchbowl three times in rapid succession. I remember thinking that we might have trouble; Mom's eggnogs were never mild. This was the first time the two opportunists had a chance to drink since I put the liquor in the storehouse.

But we were abruptly thrown into the children's world of Christmas, and I forgot about our two misfits. Mom stooped under the tree and began to pass out our presents. Most of the others had followed the pattern Cheryl and I set; nearly everything there was for a child.

While the children played on the floor under the tree, we went back to the punchbowl. "Why, it's empty!" Mom said, giggling a little—one of her eggnogs was certainly more than she could handle. I saw that Grennig and Shostovar were gone. They had finished the eggnog and gone to sleep it off—or so I thought.

"I'll have to make another batch," Mom decided, glancing at me. "Jerry, won't you let us—"

"If it's all right, Jerry," Lin Yeng put in, "I'll run over to the warehouse and get some more liquor."

I signed the withdrawal requisition and handed it to him. While he was gone, we sang carols around the piano. Half a dozen of them. Then Barbara Yeng began to look anxious.

"I don't know why he's taking so long," she said. "I'd better see if he needs any help."

She was back in five minutes, and Lin Yeng was leaning heavily on her arm. His face was bruised and bleeding; his right eye was swollen shut. Barbara helped him into a chair by the fire. While Hank Jenkins cleaned the wounds, the Chinese told us what had happened.

When he opened the door of the storehouse, Grennig and Shostovar had been inside—very drunk. They were maneuvering a case of whiskey through a broken window. Yeng went to stop them—and that was all he remembered until Barbara found him sprawled on the floor.

My immediate reaction was to go after the two men, but I reminded myself that this was a community responsibility—and I waited to see what the others would do. This was our first clear-cut criminal act.

And I wasn't let down. They reached a decision almost as a matter of course, each of them in his own way very much aware of the precedent of justice we were setting up.

Igor Morrenski said slowly, "They have taken material from our warehouse without a requisition—without even offering to do the extra work to earn it. We should make them do the work, and deprive them of what's left of the stolen liquor as a penalty."

"If they refuse—"

"Then they should have none of the other things they get by living with us. That means food and a place to sleep and our friendship."

"That's exile!" Mom cried.

"If they choose that, yes," Cheryl told her.

"What about my cousin?" Chen Phiang asked. "Do we punish them only for taking property, and not for the harm they have done him?"

"We're trying to make a world for free men," Yorovich added. "Property has a secondary place with us. Shostovar and Grennig have violated everything we believe in."

From his chair Lin Yeng spoke slowly, lisping because of his cut lip. "I think we might use two penalties. I'll miss some time from work because of what they've done. Shostovar and Grennig should make that up in general community labor. Secondly, they should be sent back to school with our kids until the teachers are satisfied that their incorrect attitudes have changed."

"With these two," Roswell reminded us, "that sentence could run forever."

"I was thinking about special classes," Lin Yeng explained. "A reading program, let's say. They might be made to spend a certain period each day with books selected by Stewart Roswell, and Roswell could give them examinations at intervals."

That settled it. Yorovich and Psorkarian were sent to bring the two men in. By that time the community accepted them as our police arm. The decision was made by the whole group acting together, with no prompting from me.

I saw our dream emerge into a still sharper reality. Cheryl was right. Christmas had been a time for the renewal of my faith.

IV. The Valley—March, The First Year

ON AN afternoon in March I rode west out of the village with Boris Yorovich to Cedar Lake, a very small, artificial lake, which had once been a motion picture, set. Since the village was wired for electricity, Yorovich had spent months trying to work out a scheme to give us power again. He had a general knowledge of electronics and he had done a great deal of technical reading during the winter. The narrow dam that made Cedar Lake had a drop of nearly thirty feet. Yorovich thought he could find material in Canster's appliance shop and build a generator to take advantage of the flow of water.

"I could use three men most of the summer, Jerry," Yorovich said.

"We can spare them. The kids will do a lot of the farm work."

"I may want more part of the time." He pointed down the gully below the dam. "I want to channel three more streams into the lake, Jerry, so we'll have a larger flow of water over the dam; it'll help prevent a freeze-up next winter."

"We should have electricity, Boris, particularly for refrigeration. I think I ought to let you have all the manpower you need."

"It's tough when we can't use Shostovar and Grennig."

"We agreed on the punishment and we'll stick it out."

That policy was the final evolution of the decision we made Christmas Eve. We gave the men their choice: exile or reform. If they chose to stay in our valley, they did so as children. At the time both of them had been hilariously amused; they weren't laughing any longer. As soon as they had done the extra labor to pay for the stolen liquor and Lin Yeng's lost time, we assigned them to the library and a special class conducted for them alone by Virginia Grant.

"It's working out," Yorovich told me. "At least for Shostovar. He's beginning to take us seriously."

"Roswell agrees with you. In any case, Boris, this is different from our old idea of criminal punishment. We could have locked the two of them up for a couple of months; this way we have a chance of changing the way they think and making them useful adults."

"What about Grennig?"

"He talks a fast line, but it's a sham; he hates us all…"

During the past three months I had read shelves of books on government; I had talked endlessly with Debby Zacharias and Stewart Roswell, picking their minds clean of ideas. I concluded that the most workable, the most man-centered government was the form I knew best—the constitutional organization of the United States.

My cigar was out. I tossed it in the fire. I stripped off

my clothes and slid down into the envelope of blankets on my cot.

Three hours later I was awakened by a frantic pounding on the door. "Derry! Derry, tome twick!" It was a child's voice, shrill with terror. I leaped out of bed, throwing a log on the dying fire as I crossed toward the door. The boy on the step was Don Harrow, the five-year-old adopted by Igor Morrenski and Emily Marsh. Don threw his arms around my neck. I carried him close to the fire. He was wearing his woolies. Snow had soaked through the cloth and the child was trembling from the cold.

"Karl Grennig's beating up my Daddy!" Don said through chattering teeth. "An' he hit my Mommy an' made her face bleed…"

The Morrenski's cottage door was open. Igor lay on the floor in front of the dying fire. I took his battered face in my hands and he seized my arm convulsively. In a choked whisper he said,

"Go after them, Jerry. He stole my wife."

"After I get you—"

"The hell with me! I'm all right. Grennig has my Emily!"

"Which road did they take?"

"East, to the desert. Grennig has one of the horses."

I ran to the corral. Psorkarian kept some small arms there. Apparently Grennig hadn't known that, for the cabinet was still locked. I opened it with my own key and took out a rifle before I mounted one of the Cossack's horses.

I rode in bleak darkness, hearing nothing but the howl of the wind. The powdery snow tore at my face like a thousand needles of ice. I was constantly bent low over the side of my horse so I could make out the trail in the snow. When I passed the four-thousand-foot marker the snow on the road was slush; a thousand feet lower it became a cold, driving rain. I had no more hoof marks to follow. If Grennig made the desert, he stood a good chance of getting away.

But there was one factor he hadn't calculated : the quixotic behavior of a mountain storm. Suddenly I was out of the rain. Moonlight stabbed down through the broiling, wind-driven clouds. I was able to see the highway ahead.

I pushed my horse faster. The advantage shifted to me. Grennig was carrying a woman; I rode alone. I cantered another mile before I came to the long slide, which the desert bombing had thrown over the road. I saw Grennig then, almost across the slide area.

I fired my rifle high above his head. I heard Emily Marsh scream as Grennig dug spurs into his horse's flank. She had been slumped across the saddle, playing unconscious until she knew someone was behind her.

She pushed herself from his horse, rolling on the asphalt. Grennig reined in his mount and went back after her.

I caught up with them as they fought on the shoulder of the highway. I swung from the saddle and prodded the German back with my rifle. He stood facing me with bared teeth. For the first time since I had known him, his eyes were neither candid nor child-like. The mask was gone and I saw the man: shrewd, savage, calculating —an ape with the cerebral cortex of a human being.

"You can go, Grennig," I said, nodding toward the desert. "You don't have a choice any longer. But Emily's going back with me, where she belongs."

"Always the Gallahad," he sneered.

I smashed his face with my fist. His eyes glazed but he held his grip on consciousness. He seized a rock and tried to hammer it into my skull. I jerked my head aside. The stone ripped a gash in my cheek with an agonizing fire of pain. I doubled my knees and kicked him from me. He groped for the rifle, lying on the road. I threw myself at him. He swung the butt of the rifle in a wide arc. It grazed my shin.

Grennig jerked back the bolt as I struck him with my shoulder. We both went down and the rifle was between us. The explosion was muffled by our bodies. I saw the look of surprise in his face—and the slow emptiness of death...

V. The City and the Valley—November, The Second Year

BY NOVEMBER—a year and a half after the war began—the population in the valley had grown to two hundred and fifty. I no longer felt any doubt. Some men had understood George Knight. We all would in time.

Yet there was always one question in my mind. Our greatest opportunity had been Los Angeles. Knight's broadcasts had been made primarily to the city. But Los Angeles chose war. Why?

In November we set up our first formal government and we held our first election. I was chosen president by a vote of two hundred and twenty. Thirty of our children, defined as still socially immature, did not vote.

We held our election late in the afternoon, and afterward Cheryl and I walked up to the knoll above the lake. I felt a need to be alone with her, and the others understood that.

Cheryl and I sat together, looking at the lake in silence.

The sun was setting and the fall wind was bitter with the first icy touch of winter. Cheryl moved closer to me. She slid her hand beneath my shirt to keep it warm. I felt the gentle touch of her finger tracing the muscle of my chest— her favorite, almost unconscious gesture of affection. I remembered that on this knoll we first found our love for each other; I drew her face toward mine. She lay in my arms with her lips soft and liquid on my cheek.

Far away I heard the sound of sudden gunfire. I pushed Cheryl from me. On the village street someone was screaming.

I sprinted toward the village. Yorovich came out of the lodge and tossed me one of our submachine guns. The street was in chaos. Our citizens were scurrying into the shelter of the empty stores. Bearded strangers on horseback were riding up and down the road, firing rifles into the mob.

Yorovich and I opened up on the horsemen. Four flung up their hands and fell in the street. The others retreated to the eastern end of the village and barricaded themselves in an empty building. Yorovich and I pinned them down long enough for our people to take cover and our men to break out their guns.

"It's men from the city," Yorovich said.

"After food, you think?"

"Obviously. Winter's coming. There isn't much left to pillage anywhere else."

"We could buy them off with the canned goods we don't need. But to hell with that."

"You're right, Jerry. You can't buy peace from the savages. We fight it out right now, or they'll destroy us sooner or later."

When dusk came, we were attacked by a second force,

which had lain outside the village. The men escaped from the barricaded store and the two groups formed a united front against us. The fighting was continuous until nearly dawn. Our superior weapons eventually forced them to retreat.

We rested after the night's fighting until noon before we set out in pursuit of the invaders. Fifty of us went in our two big diesel vans.

Our war against the barbarians was short-lived and very one-sided. Although we faced an enemy outnumbering us five to one, we had superior weapons—and Psorkarian, in the helicopter, gave us an air force. By late afternoon we had taken nearly sixty prisoners.

The brigand stronghold had been the undamaged mansions on the ocean boulevard overlooking Los Angeles harbor. We were still rounding up four prisoners on the beach below the bluff, when the helicopter swung low overhead and Psorkarian called out my name.

"Yes, Cossack?" I shouted up to him. "What is it?"

"A ship of some sort, Jerry. Just outside the breakwater."

"Armed?"

"Damned if I know. I never saw anything like this before."

An hour later I understood what he meant. The monstrosity maneuvered through the harbor entrance, past the flattop sunk against the breakwater, and moved toward the beach. It was a box-like raft with a sail. The sail was a crazy patchwork of varicolored cloth hitched together with woven palm fronds. Along each side of the raft a super-structure held hand-carved oars which six men were plying. The thing stopped fifty feet offshore.

From the deck of the raft a man shouted at us, "Who

are you?"

"Americans," I answered.

"You survived in the city?"

"No; we're from the hills."

"We're looking for a man. You may have heard of him—Jerry Bonhill."

"Why?"

"He broadcast to the city. He told us how—"

"I'm Bonhill! come ashore."

The raft ground on the beach. The man sprang ashore and shook my hand eagerly. He was emaciated, gray-bearded, yet still very distinguished looking. His face had been tanned leather-brown by the sun and the wind. He told me his name was Maurice Phelps, of the U. S. Navy.

He described the destruction of Los Angeles. The navy, he said, had entered the harbor without opposition. All day long, before the attack, they had been hearing broadcasts which began, "I am Jerry Bonhill; I am speaking for George Knight." At first they thought it was a trick, but Soviet sailors in the submarines —sick men, barely able to stand—welcomed them as friends.

However, the Soviet commander had a hard-core defense of about three thousand men—out of the quarter million in the city. Russian planes bombed the incoming ships; the navy drove them off. As the Angelinos and their sick captors moved toward the harbor, the Russians bombed the city indiscriminately with explosives and incendiary bombs. The navy attempted to evacuate both civilians and friendly Soviet troops. The first wave of sick men was loaded into Phelps' ship, and he was ordered to take them to Catalina.

Phelps' ship was in the channel, five miles west of the breakwater, when the sound of firing suddenly stopped in the city. On the horizon they could see the flames of the burning city, but Phelps remembered hearing the motor of only one plane soaring over the ruins.

Ten minutes after that Phelps' ship exhausted its last reserve of fuel. He had no choice but to drop anchor. Half an hour later a Russian submarine surfaced close to Phelps' ship. Ten Russian sailors asked to come aboard—emaciated by the radiation sickness; a terrible horror in their eyes. They were the last men who escaped the city. They had been aboard the submarine when they heard ashore the cry of "Gas!" Instinctively they slammed the hatches and submerged. Through the periscope they saw the people on the landing fall dead. They saw the ships one by one go out of control. They watched the war-god in the gas mask slaughter a city. The last city of man, which Knight's dream had almost saved.

Since the submarine had the almost inexhaustible power of atomic engines, Phelps used it to make repeated trips ferrying his men and the refugees to Catalina Island. Approximately half the men aboard his ship were Communist troops; the other evacuees were Americans who insisted on sticking by the sick enemy they were trying to help. "A remarkable display of courage," Phelps admitted. "But the whole city was like that; the spiritual excitement of a Crusade. All of them talked constantly about Knight."

The sea was running high and on its last trip back to the ship the submarine, manned by an exhausted crew, rammed it. Both vessels began to sink. Phelps and the fifteen seamen still aboard went ashore on a life raft. The island was a shambles, swept by fire.

"Our first year out there was rugged, Bonhill—pure hell. Half of us died of the sickness and starvation. But through it all we never forgot those broadcasts to the city. It gave us something beyond ourselves to work for. We had the Russians with us; we saw what it meant to teach them the meaning of America—our revolution, in place of the Communist sham."

During the second summer they managed to grow a little food, but the Catalina colony had existed close to starvation. Fish was their staple diet; but the spirit of George Knight kept them alive.

The refugees had spent a good part of the summer building Phelps' raft. The old life raft, which they had used for fishing, was in no condition to make the passage to the mainland. Before another winter came, they wanted to leave the island. Phelps and his six sailors had come to find a larger ship, which would be capable of moving the whole colony. Like the Wawona refugees, they surmised that I might have built a colony like theirs. They were ready to join forces. I told him they would be welcome to the valley, and I explained how much progress we had made toward rebuilding an organized society.

"So it's President Bonhill." He said it with an embarrassing reverence. "The first President of the American world—for the new breed of American. You'll find us everywhere. In Russia and Africa. In Brazil and Ireland. It is our world, Bonhill; we won't lose it again."

Phelps and his six sailors examined the ships in the harbor. They found what they could use. We worked half the night helping them drain fuel from other rusting hulks to fill the tanks of that one vessel. They sailed immediately. Phelps thought he could land his Catalina colony in Los Angeles shortly after dawn.

I lay awake a long time looking at the stars, hazy above the coastal mists. I felt an inner peace and satisfaction; the last question mark was gone. George Knight had not failed in Los Angeles. One man had destroyed the city, yet even here Knight's dream had not died.

At seven the next morning, when the thin, wasted survivors of the Catalina colony came ashore, our trucks were waiting on the road above the beach. It was a three-hour drive up the road to the valley. I sat with the driver in the cab of one of the trucks; the pale, gaunt people crowded in the van behind us were singing as we moved over the highways of the dead city.

When we reached the village the air was crisp and cold. Snow clouds were scattered over the sky. Our citizens welcomed the newcomers soberly, as friends and as brothers. They took them in and fed them.

I walked back to our cabin with Cheryl. The afternoon sun blazed through the windows. Our first winter fire burned on the hearth.

I dropped on the couch beside Cheryl. "The prisoners Yorovich brought in," she said. "I thought if we put them—"

"We have an elected government, Cheryl. The responsibility isn't all ours any longer." I put my arm around her. "It seems to me we were interrupted yesterday—"

"And it isn't right for the President to leave unfinished business. It sets a bad precedent for our children."

Her fingers worked at the buttons of my shirt. I felt her hand caress my chest and move slowly toward the small of my back.

"Never a new world," I murmured in her ear. "A man and a woman together—they found it long ago."

She sighed and then, crooning deep-throatedly, she

whispered Solomon's song, the ancient magic of love,

"Behold, thou art fair, my beloved... The beams of our house are cedar, and our rafters of fir.'"

And after that she had no more time for words.

THE END

If you've enjoyed this book, you will not want to miss these terrific titles…

ARMCHAIR SCI-FI, & HORROR DOUBLE NOVELS, $12.95 each

D-21   **EMPIRE OF EVIL** by Robert Arnette
THE SIGN OF THE TIGER by Alan E. Nourse & J. A. Meyer

D-22   **OPERATION SQUARE PEG** by Frank Belknap Long
ENCHANTRESS OF VENUS by Leigh Brackett

D-23   **THE LIFE WATCH** by Lester Del Rey
CREATURES OF THE ABYSS by Murray Leinster

D-24   **BLACK MAGIC HOLIDAY** by Robert Bloch
STAR HUNTER   by Andre Norton

D-25   **EMPIRE OF WOMEN** by John Fletcher
ONE OF OUR CITIES IS MISSING by Irving Cox

D-26   **THE WRONG SIDE OF PARADISE** by Raymond F. Jones
THE INVOLUNTARY IMMORTALS by Rog Phillips

D-27   **EARTH QUARTER** by Damon Knight
ENVOY TO NEW WORLDS by Keith Laumer

D-28   **SLAVES TO THE METAL HORDE** by Milton Lesser
HUNTERS OUT OF TIME by Joseph E. Kelleam

D-29   **RX JUPITER SAVE US** by Ward Moore
BEWARE THE USURPERS by Geoff St. Reynard

D-30   **SECRET OF THE SERPENT** by Don Wilcox
CRUSADE ACROSS THE VOID by Dwight V. Swain

ARMCHAIR SCIENCE FICTION CLASSICS, $12.95 each

C-7   **THE SHAVER MYSTERY, pt. 1**
by Richard S. Shaver

C-8   **THE SHAVER MYSTERY, pt. 2**
by Richard S. Shaver

C-9   **MURDER IN SPACE** by David V. Reed
by David V. Reed

ARMCHAIR MASTERS OF SCIENCE FICTION SERIES, $16.95 each

M-3   **MASTERS OF SCIENCE FICTION, Vol. Three**
Robert Sheckley

M-4   **MASTERS OF SCIENCE FICTION, Vol. Four**
Mack Reynolds, part one